IN YOUR DREAMS

Lynn Bulock

A KISMET™ Romance

METEOR PUBLISHING CORPORATION

Bensalem, Pennsylvania

To Joe, always.
To Barbara, for giving me wings.
To Evan, for believing.
To Kate, for the magic.

LYNN BULOCK

Lynn Bulock is the author of seven contemporary romances and several children's stories. She lives in St. Peters, Missouri, with her husband and two sons. When she isn't writing, she's usually reading, or thinking about writing, or chauffeuring somebody to an activity while thinking about writing, which is why her house looks the way it does.

To Her Glory

To love, give, and nurture and ...
To serve, lend, share ...
To know, to life, to laugh.

DEAR DIARY

PROLOGUE

"Okay, Mutt, here we go. Easy now." Alex pushed open the door to Meg Shepherd's dormitory room. His other arm still cradled her close to him, supporting her. Meg thought she'd never felt anything that felt as good as that firm shoulder behind her. It sure kept the room from whirling. "Where's Cindi?"

"Gone home. I'm alllllll alone," Meg said, enjoying the sound of her voice bouncing off the cinder block walls. "All alone except for you, Alex."

"Yeah, well, now that you're home safe you're going to be all alone, Mutt. See you tomorrow. You have any aspirin?"

She looked up at him, wondering why there was that glitter in those deep blue eyes. Midnight sky and stars, that's what it looked like, Meg thought. He had asked her a question, hadn't he? Alex, looking down, seemed to expect an answer. If the funny fog created by all that beer at the party would just part for a minute, maybe she could answer him.

Aspirin. He wanted an aspirin. "You have a head-ache, Alex?" She reached up a hand and traced it through the thick, wavy mass of deep gold at his temple.

Alex chuckled, that deep throaty sound she loved so much. "No, little one, but you sure will have tomorrow. Do you have any aspirin?"

"Sure. Somewhere." Her hand in his hair seemed to be affecting Alex as much as it was her. He turned his head into her hand, kissing the palm softly. The feel of his lips made Meg shiver, as always. "How come that happens, Alex?" Maybe he had the answer to the mystery. He seemed to know everything else.

"What do you mean?" He gently removed her hand from his hair and guided her over to her bed, sitting her down in one easy motion.

"That tingly stuff," she said, reaching out to draw him down. "You're too high to talk to up there. Makes my neck stiff. Come down here."

"I can't. You lock your door behind me and go to sleep, Mutt, okay? And sleep with one foot on the floor. It keeps the room from spinning. Why'd you drink that much anyway, Mutt?"

"You were."

His hand was caressing her hair, and the action made Meg think of someone comforting a very small child. "I'm used to it," he said. "And you didn't have to try to match me drink for drink, anyway. I'm a whole lot bigger than you are."

"Sure are." Meg grinned. Alex was like a wall, a solid, comforting wall. Except walls didn't have such delightfully sculptured chests under their white shirts. And walls didn't bend down and kneel in front of her, putting hands on her shoulders.

"Mutt, you need to go to sleep now. You going to be okay?"

Meg thought it over, looking into those midnight eyes again. "No. I can't do the buttons."

"Buttons," Alex repeated.

She turned away from him to demonstrate. "Oooh, that makes the room move again. But see, Alex. Buttons."

There were dozens of them, all the way down the back of the delicate pastel creation she had worn to the fraternity party. After all, the winners of the all-campus bed race had to look good in victory, didn't they?

Alex certainly had. The white shirt and the pressed, tailored wool slacks fit him to perfection. But then everything did. Meg marveled daily at the way he made even his worn everyday jeans look wonderful.

At the moment he seemed at a loss for words. "You want me to undo these? All of them, Mutt?"

"I can't sleep in this dress, Alex. It would get all . . . squashed. I can't squash my new dress, because I wasn't even supposed to buy it in the first place."

"I'll bet. Daddy's going to squawk when he sees the charge bill, isn't he?" Alex sounded grim.

Meg tried to wave away whatever was bothering him. "He'll never see it. I'll take care of that. But I cannot squash my dress."

Alex sighed. "Okay. Lift that hair out of the way then."

Obediently, Meg lifted the mass of strawberry-blond curls. She could feel Alex's long, agile fingers start on the row of tiny cloth buttons.

The first few tickled, especially the one right over the bone at the base of her neck. It was hard to suppress a giggle. "Dammit, Mutt, this is hard enough," Alex said. His voice sounded strained. "Don't you dare wiggle."

"I'm not wiggling," she said with as much gravity as she could muster. His hands traveled lower, still working. It was so quiet in the room that Meg could hear the spring noises outside the slightly open window, mixed with a song from someone's stereo on the floor above them.

Alex leaned his forehead against her back. "Are you sure you can't do this?" Meg could feel the smooth skin against hers. He seemed to be sweating.

She reached her hands back. They weren't working very well, not in the middle of her back like that. And reaching that way made the room start moving again. "Nope. Won't work. Are there that many more?"

"Dozens. And every one is a little harder. . . ." Alex trailed off.

"Should be easier," Meg argued. "See, it's almost coming off." She shrugged her shoulders and the wide poufs of chintz that made up the sleeves of the dress slid away, leaving it clinging only by the rest of the buttons down her back.

"Aw, don't do that, Mutt." Alex seemed to groan as Meg slipped out of the sleeves, congratulating herself for doing something on her own.

"You asked me to help," she argued.

"I did." He kept working on the buttons doggedly. Meg could feel the heat of his breath on the sensitive skin of her back and wondered why his breathing was so ragged. He was unfastening the last ten or so of the buttons now, down low on her spine. Meg had never felt anything as delicious as his hands there.

Forgetting the consequences of sudden movement, she slipped out of his grasp and stood by the bed. The dress slid to the floor in a whisper of fabric and collapsed in a heap around her feet. "There." Meg tried to hop out of the puddle of clothing, but the room wasn't cooperating. It decided to move again, tilting everything crazily. She dived for Alex's arms, and he caught her before she fell.

The spinning stopped as she closed her eyes. In its place was another kind of dizziness, one she suspected had much to do with the fact that Alex Langdon's strong young body was so close to her. She could feel the length of his thighs along her legs, and up where the silky fabric of her bra separated her skin from him, his chest rose and fell rapidly.

He had a sweet, sharp male smell and Meg lowered her head to inhale more of it. Her hands slid around his neck, tracing the taut muscles in his back under his shirt. Her move brought a tightening of his arms wrapped around her. Alex burrowed his warm mouth into the soft spot where her bra hooked in the front. "Oh, Alex." Her voice sounded as if she was in church, and that was the kind of awe Meg felt.

Alex sounded as if he were going to strangle. "We have to get you to bed, Mutt."

"Yes," she whispered. "We do." She could not imagine anything sweeter than this moment unless it was the moments that would surely follow.

"No, baby, alone." Alex tried to pull away, but her hands came up, burying themselves in that thatch of hair.

"No, Alex. Stay. The room doesn't move when you hold me."

"I wish it were that simple. The room moving is the least of your worries if I stay, Mutt." His words were unbelievably warm against her skin.

"Please?" Pleading didn't come easily, but Meg couldn't think of anything she'd ever wanted more.

Alex made a sound that started out a soft sigh and ended up a groan against her skin. "Come on, then. I'll try."

They ended up with Alex against the wall, propped up by her pillows. Meg snuggled against the length of him and sighed contentedly. "Slide that foot out of here, Mutt. I'm serious. If you put one foot on the floor, the room won't move."

"All right." She shifted on her hip, trying to get her lower leg to cooperate and find the floor. The move put her in contact with Alex, the base of her neck at his collarbone, with her back feeling the long length of him down to her ankle.

She gasped at all the sensations the move created. This close, there was no denying what this position was costing him as well. Meg turned into him, pressing even closer to him when his mouth came down on top of hers, hungry but still incredibly gentle.

Meg couldn't get close enough to him. There was too much between them, their clothing, the sheet he'd insisted she slide under. Still, she had to breathe. She shuddered with the intake of air. "Oh, Alex, please? Can't we?"

The sound that came out of him, buried in her neck, was almost a sob. "You are so drunk, Mutt. This can't be happening."

"It is happening. And in the morning I'll be sober, Alex," she said, starting to unbutton his shirt.

"Then in the morning we'll . . . go on from here," he said, holding both of her hands. "In the morning, all right?"

"In the morning," she echoed. Suddenly the effort was all too much. Meg was aware of Alex's releasing her hands and turning her gently away from him as she drifted off.

"Alex?"

"What, Mutt?"

"You'll really be here, in the morning?"

"Really."

In the morning her head hurt even before she lifted it. And someone seemed to have poured a bottle of glue into her mouth while she slept. Glue made of old horses' hooves, apparently. Meg put her hand on the cool windowsill next to the bed and sat up.

"I hope you're feeling better than I am," she said, opening her eyes and expecting to see Alex's bulk at the end of the bed.

Her bed was empty except for the tangle of covers she'd created herself. There wasn't even an imprint left of the warm male body she sought. Cindi's bed hadn't been slept in either. Alex was gone and had been for some time.

Leaning against the window frame, Meg looked out, gulping the cool morning air. The corner of the screen gave when she pressed against it, as if someone had popped it out of its frame and slid it back in. And in front of the window, on the soft spring earth, were two footprints. They looked like the mark of someone who'd leaped out the window in a hurry.

Meg slammed the window shut and flung herself out of bed, ignoring the hideous, queasy pounding the movement set up in her head. So he'd stay, would he? They'd go on from there in the morning? Meg had never felt more abandoned and humiliated in her entire life.

It was apparent where Alex had gone. Away, anywhere to get away from the unappealing drunken little twit she'd made of herself last night. He'd gone out the window rather than face her.

Meg grabbed a towel and her container of toiletries to head down to the showers. She couldn't confront him like this. She looked down. She couldn't even go to the showers like this, in her bra and slip. A hot blush stained her cheeks when she thought of standing plastered against Alex like this, while Alex thought of ways to shut her up and get her to sleep so that he could leave.

She snatched a robe from the hook next to the

closet and threw it on. A shower, a cold one, to clear her head. Then she would dress and go in search of Alex. This time of the morning on a Sunday, she knew exactly where to find him. And when she did, she knew exactly what she would do.

ONE

The old panic was back, rising in icy tingles from Meg Shepherd's spine, squeezing the breath out of her lungs. She thought she had left it behind a long time ago, but in the teasing April breeze tugging at tendrils of her strawberry-blond hair, she shivered. It wasn't the cool of the wind that made the back of her neck tense. It was the rising feeling that she was making a terrible mistake.

From her seat in the middle tiers of Busch Memorial Stadium Meg had a wonderful view of the game. The figures dancing around on the bright green Astroturf were so clear she could see the expressions on their faces. If she could pay attention to the game, she might be enjoying herself.

At least if she paid attention, she might have something to tell Gabe when she got back to the hospital. Of course, he was probably watching the game on television. He'd understand those strange signals the coach was exchanging with the base runners. And if his heart was pounding, it was only because his hero did something right from the pitcher's mound.

Meg's heart, however, didn't care about pitchers. It was threatening to climb up her throat at the thought that she might run into Alex Langdon. That was nonsense, she told herself. The man had a job to do, and if he was at this game, he was up in a press box somewhere, reporting.

She could imagine him, up in the tier of closed boxes above her. His tie would be gone, shirt collar open on that magnificent neck that still taunted her every night during the sports portion of the news. At a game his deep golden hair would be rumpled from his unconscious habit of running his fingers through it, instead of carefully styled, as it was in the newspaper picture next to his column, the one that still gave her a moment of breathing difficulty if she came upon it unaware in one of the hospital waiting rooms.

There was a crack of ball on bat and the people around Meg joined the murmur of excitement running through the stadium. She pushed away the fruitless thoughts of Alex and tried to concentrate on the game.

It made more sense than worrying if she was going to run into him today. Granted, working less than five miles from each other in the same city guaranteed that it would happen sooner or later. But not today. If he hadn't contacted her in the six months he'd been here, it wasn't going to happen today. Meg picked imaginary lint off her skirt, fidgeting.

Maybe she wouldn't run into Alex but would just

manage to mess things up all by herself. She did seem to have that talent at times. Still, she'd managed this right so far. It looked as if she was going to get Gabriel his meeting with this pitcher, Masterson, without doing anything but calling in one favor owed from the *Morning Star* sports desk.

It had only taken one walk through her card file to discover that Doug from the *Star* was the one she'd hunted up an orthopedic specialist for, to finish his story on shin splints two weeks ago. Then one call to Doug, or at least his replacement on the desk, had gotten her good tickets to the game and a promise that Masterson would be in the locker room, expecting her.

She moved to the edge of the seat so that she could rest her toes on the concrete floor under the tier of seats. Crossing and uncrossing her feet at the ankles, she moistened her lips again and looked at the scoreboard. One and a half more innings until she went into the lions' den. She wondered if she'd live that long, or if anxiety would smother her first.

"This is ridiculous," she muttered, looking out at the playing field again. She was a grown woman. Why was the thought of walking into a locker room full of baseball players and talking to one man making her feel as though she was getting ready to jump out of an airplane?

She reached into her pocket and fingered the slick plastic hospital I.D. badge like a talisman. It felt funny in her hand. Meg hadn't used it outside the hospital since it had been issued when she started work there. Usually, other people came to her for this sort of thing. She didn't go to them.

As a public relations staffer at Mercy Children's Hospital in St. Louis, she had a pretty succinct job description. It didn't entail holding hands of patients or their parents. She was supposed to be at the hospital to write press releases and brief the media, nice sterile stuff like that. But once in a while a patient breached the wall between her and the reality of what she was writing those press releases about.

Gabe Kincaid had been that way from the first. The radio and television stations had called for more information the minute they'd gotten wind of his story, but the Kincaids were having none of it. Gabe wanted no publicity. He maintained that anybody would have done what he had. Meg wondered how many people would have thrown themselves under several tons of machinery, even for their own cousin.

Gabe might not have done it himself if he had known the cost. Meg had seen him, white-faced with pain while the nurses changed the dressings on the burns one more time or attended to skin grafts. She'd watched him silent through repair of the damaged muscle and bone that had survived the terrible injury.

Her mother would have said she was taking in strays again if she'd told her about Gabe. So she hadn't, agonizing alone instead over what she could do for the young man.

Of course, she hadn't known the answer would mean fighting a panic attack in a crowded stadium. Maybe she wouldn't have offered if she'd known that. Still, Gabe would give his good leg to meet "Dat" Masterson, so here she was.

Still, she had to be crazy to be doing this. Her palms were getting moist, and she raked them down the nubby linen of her skirt. For the hundredth time Meg wished she'd brought her sunglasses. Then maybe she wouldn't be squinting while she tried to read the scoreboard.

Bottom of the eighth inning. Almost time to go down to the locker room. Meg couldn't stand sitting here waiting among strangers any longer. She left her seat, leaving behind the crumpled, nearly full, peanut package, and the scorecard she hadn't touched. She still couldn't figure one out. In her mind, Alex laughed. "Yes, I'm still a sports illiterate," she muttered to herself to stop the mocking laughter that was as clear as if he were really standing beside her.

Walking down the concrete steps, into the maze of ramps and snack stands and souvenir vendors, Meg wondered why his image wouldn't leave her alone. Surely by now she should be able to banish him. Whatever she'd once felt for Alex Langdon, it should be long gone.

Should be was the operative phrase here, Meg told herself as she pushed open the door to the ladies' room and went straight for the mirror. The pins weren't taming the riot of strawberry-blond curls as well as they had before. She tucked a stray curl up into the loose coil on the back of her neck, glad that she'd thought about the wind in the stadium. Her mouth was dry, and her lips felt tight when she pressed them together. Rummaging in her purse, she found her lipstick. She swiped another bit of pink across her mouth. It was still awfully wide, but at least it was covered. Too bad she couldn't cover the freckles.

Meg moved back one step and gave herself a judicious once-over. She wasn't sure what sports reporters usually looked like, but she suspected she was a far cry from their typical appearance. Still, she liked this suit, in its sassy shade of plum. The contrast of color with the jacket always made her eyes look greener. Feeling good had to count for something, and this suit made her feel good.

She took a deep breath and headed down to the lower levels of the stadium. Things looked different down here, away from the crowd. It was like being in a giant concrete maze. More than ever she felt like a panicked hamster, and she pushed back the feeling.

She passed a bank of pay phones and stopped. On impulse she walked back toward them, fishing in her purse for change. Two rings and then an answer. "Room 312." Gabe's voice sounded distracted. In the background she could hear the game.

"Hi, sport. I don't have to ask what you're doing," she said, trying to sound cheerful.

"Hi, Meg. Where are you? I missed you at lunch. They had your favorite, green rubber Jell-O."

"Yum. I'm sorry I had other plans," she said. Just hearing his voice gave Meg the strength to will her knees to keep from knocking. He was the reason she was doing this. This young man full of enthusiasm and humor, who should be going to baseball games instead of sitting in a hospital bed, who should be practicing for a season of Legion ball instead of undergoing skin grafts. She had to do something for him.

"Other plans for sure. I can tell you're not in your office. You sound like you're in a tunnel or something."

"Close. I'm in the stadium," she admitted.

"Aw, man, some people have all the luck. Bring me some peanuts, okay? And your scorecard."

Meg laughed. "It's blank."

There was silence. "You're kidding. Even when Masterson struck out all three in the seventh?"

"Even there. I'll bring it to you anyway, if you want," Meg said.

"Fine. I bet I can fill it out from memory."

"I bet you can. I'll see you later, okay?"

" 'Kay." Gabe hung up and Meg put the phone receiver back on its hook. She looked down, wishing she had worn flats. That trek back up to her seat would take just about all the time until the players got into the locker room. It couldn't be helped, though. She had a scorecard to rescue. Sighing, she headed back up the ramp.

At the locker room, a few media people were milling in and out. Meg clutched the plastic pass, reminding herself to look professional. The guard checked her name on a list and waved her in without a second glance. Inside, the team areas weren't any more glamorous than the concrete outside. Meg looked around to see if she could see Masterson, hoping she would recognize him from his pictures.

After sitting with Gabe these last few weeks, she knew everything about Michael "Bat" Masterson except his brief size. Gabe probably knew that. Meg craned her neck, wishing for more height than even the three-inch heels of her pumps gave her. She was still shorter than the crowd here.

There were lots of sweaty guys in red and white uniforms, but none who looked like Masterson. Most were surrounded by one or two people, usually men, with microphones or notebooks. All seemed absorbed in their conversations and paid no attention to Meg.

She finally caught one player's eye. "Hi, I'm looking for Mike Masterson," she said, trying to sound cheerful and businesslike. "I'm supposed to meet him here."

Sure you are, the man's eyes said. He looked around briefly, shrugged, and was already walking away as he answered. "Sorry, don't see him."

These guys were rude. Meg pocketed her pass and looked for another player, or maybe even a manager or someone who looked like he knew what he was doing.

Plenty of guys looked like they knew what they were doing, but none of them would look at her. Instead of attracting attention by being short and female, Meg almost seemed invisible. Nobody would talk to her. The room was beginning to clear out and Meg couldn't find anyone who knew where Masterson was. Her palms were still sweating and she could feel one curl coming down the back of her neck. But now anger was replacing the panic in a warm, fiery glow she could feel on her cheeks. "This is a conspiracy," she muttered to herself, suppressing the urge to curse. There had to be somebody who could direct her to Masterson.

She wasn't going to get this far and go back to tell Gabe she'd blown it. There were still too many tricks she could use from her old arsenal. Alex's training had come in handy more than once. Perhaps it would today. Meg looked around the room again. In a corner she spotted a cameraman loading equipment into a large canvas bag.

He was large and bulky, with the requisite billed cap and athletic jacket. Meg could only see the back of him as he bent over his equipment bag, and she hoped that was to his advantage. If there really was some sort of fraternity here that she was being kept out of, maybe an offhanded question to a distracted person would get her an answer.

It was worth a try. Meg strode up to the back of the man. She thought about tapping him on the back, but in his position it would probably startle him. Besides, he was very tall, and the portion of his denim-clad anatomy that was at tapping height looked tempting but was not what she'd usually think of tapping.

In fact, Meg's reaction to that anatomy startled her. It looked *definitely* tappable. Her panic rose up again, with giggles behind it. She had been single and alone way too long if any large male in tight jeans looked this attractive. Still, she would love to have time to trace the stitching on those pockets.

After this she would take a couple of days of vacation, she promised herself. She obviously needed the rest, but right now she had work to do.

"I'm looking for Masterson. Know where he is?" she asked, trying to sound nonchalant.

The cameraman stayed hunkered down over his bag. He didn't even turn around. "Sure. Down that hall and first door there. Can't miss him." His voice was muffled by his headfirst stance over the equipment bag. He used one arm to point in the direction of the room, still jamming things into his sack.

Victory at last. Meg took off quickly before anybody could stop her. "Thanks," she called over her shoulder. She listened to her heels click an echoing tattoo on the tile floor of the hall. The door was closed, but it wasn't locked.

"Here goes nothing," she said, eyes closed. The back of her neck felt prickly, and when she breathed in quickly, the air felt sharp. Meg pushed with one palm on the cold metal and walked through quickly before she lost her nerve.

Meg didn't know what she expected, but this wasn't it. She wasn't in an office or a room full of coolers and snacks. There was no kindly old team physician taping anybody up. There was a lot of steam and white tile and towels on the floor. Too late to chicken out now. "I'm looking for Mike Masterson. I need to talk to him. Is he here?" Meg tried to sound businesslike. Her voice echoed off the tiled walls of the room, bouncing back at her.

"In the flesh," someone said loudly. Meg followed the voice to the corner of the room, through the litter of towels and uniform parts on the floor. Suddenly Meg realized where she was, but it was too late to back off. It could be worse, she told herself. It could be the showers.

The warm, moist air swirled around her, and Meg felt rooted to the ground. Somewhere one of the men in the room hooted. "Hey, babe, you're a lot better lookin' than the regular reporters from the pool. What'd they send you over for?"

"I'm not a reporter. I'm . . . I'm from the children's hospital and I'm looking for Mike Masterson," Meg said, forcing herself to look over in the corner where the voices were coming from.

The steam was thick, but it wasn't that thick. It didn't hide Masterson, facing her in the whirlpool. He wore a grin, very brief red trunks, and some sort of elastic bandage around one knee. The detached part of Meg's brain, the part where the warning bells and panic buttons weren't whooping, said that he was probably pretty cute, with that country-boy smile. Two more men were in the whirlpool with him, their backs to Meg.

"Bat's over here," one of them called over his shoulder, his skin shedding drops of water as he shifted in the whirlpool. "No need to be shy. Come on over and talk to the man. I'll even give you my seat." He broke into a grin and hoisted himself up to the rim of the tub.

Meg still stood where she was, aware of all kinds of things swirling in her head. She could feel a blush to end all blushes crawling up from the neckline of her suit and heading posthaste for her hairline. There

was a sort of whirring behind her and a little laughter
eddying through the draft from the now open door.
And the man who'd offered her his seat was getting
up to do just that. Meg realized with a jolt that what
she'd first taken for tan briefs were made not of
cloth, just a paler strip of flesh.

Finally her feet would move. Meg started a slow
backing up from the tub and its occupants. All of
them were smiling broadly. Masterson hadn't said
another word, and he looked as if he was suppressing
a laugh. Meg kept backing up, toward the safety of
the door. The other player was still getting out of
the steaming water, and there was no doubt that he
was in a completely natural state. Meg stepped on a
towel and her heel skidded on the cloth and the slip-
pery floor. She gave an involuntary yelp.

"Come on, let me help you over here," the
friendly player called. He started to throw one leg
over the tub rim.

Before he turned, she moved. "No, that's fine.
I'll come back later. Or wait outside. Or something." She whirled through the open door and
closed it behind her with a whump. Behind the door
the players whooped with laughter. Leaning on the
door, Meg drew in the cool air of the hallway for a
split second before the lights went off in her face.

There was a roar of masculine laughter as Meg
realized she'd just had her picture taken several
times, including on videotape. So that was the familiar whir she'd heard behind her. With a sinking in
her stomach, it dawned on Meg that this had all the
feel of a setup.

The door was still behind her, and Meg was beginning to focus. The first thing that came into plain view was a piece of white paper taped to the hallway just at her eye level. On it, in large, bold handwriting with arcing loops were four words.

MUTT,

I GOTCHA

JEFF

Meg suppressed the words that came to mind first. In the laughter she could now hear a familiar roar, deep and throaty. Hearing the laughter made her response to that "cameraman" in faded denim understandable. She wasn't going crazy after all, unless wanting to commit murder counted. But in this crowd she couldn't find her intended victim. She knew she wouldn't, either.

Meg balled a fist and pounded on the door behind her. "Alex. Alex Langdon," she screamed. "I'm going to kill you."

THE MORNING STAR   SECTION D
                COMMENTARY
                Alex Langdon

There is much speculation this morning as to why one M. Margaret Shepherd went into the whirlpool room under Busch Stadium yesterday. Speculation ranges from the sublime (she was an ardent fan who merely lost her way and stumbled into the Batman in his bat briefs) to the ridiculous (she is a tabloid reporter in search of the ultimate scoop). I am here to tell you that the lady is exactly what she claims, a hospital PR person. So what was she doing in the bowels of the stadium? Simple. Mutt Shepherd entered that whirlpool because five years ago she ruined my only suit jacket.

Still with me? It gets complicated, but no more complicated than figuring batting averages. Back when I was young and foolish, I decided to help out the less fortunate. I adopted an underclassman in the national communications society, Alpha Epsilon Rho.

Other seniors got little brothers or sisters who idolized them. I got a spotted imp from hell.

Perhaps that's putting things a bit strongly. I mean, maybe other people's AERho sponsors put up with chocolate-covered raisins in their tape recorders. I'm sure that for most of them bailing their charges out of technical assignments because they couldn't reach the top row of video equipment was routine. Of course, I loved every minute of it. And Mutt's gratitude was touching. She thanked me in so many appropriate ways, like the rubber snake in my equipment bag.

Of course, there were benefits. Where else would I have gotten to explain the hot stove league to someone who wondered if they used gas or electric? There was always the challenge of finding language simple enough to elucidate for Mutt the intricacies of NFL playoff berths. I figured if I could get a concept past her, I'd put the piece on my audition tape, because any fool could understand what I was saying.

Finally, I finished that audition tape. After four years of student loans and living on cheese and crackers, I was ready for The Big One. I got an appointment with the sports director of the television station I'd watched for four years solid, swearing all the while that he was the man whose job I was going to take.

I was ready, too. I knew all my stuff, had a fresh haircut, and looked like a million dollars. My one and only suit was cleaned and pressed and I even had a clean handkerchief.

I strutted into the offices of my employer, the campus radio station, the day before the interview and posed for photos. After a hard morning's work with my shirtsleeves rolled up, feeling very much the reporter, I got ready. The tie went back on, the coat was unshrined and rebuttoned. I sat down in the booth to do the noon newscast. There seemed to be an audience outside the viewing window, impressed by my sartorial splendor.

It was here that fate intervened in the person of Mutt Shepherd. Sweet child that she was, she came in to give me moral support. Except that she came with a lighter, and instead of blowing me a kiss as I went on the air over a three-county area, she touched the lighter, ever so gently, to the corner of my newscast.

Five minutes of air copy smoked, curled, and vanished before my eyes as I finished the second line. Mutt danced out of the booth, the wisps of smoke trailing her, convincing me that she was, indeed, a demon.

Dead air was the cardinal sin on the student radio station. I could walk out now and kill her, and lose my job. Or I could deposit the smoldering newscast in the metal wastecan beside me, ignore the rubes hooting outside the window, and fake it.

I have no idea what I said for five minutes. It must have been all right, because my prose was not what alerted the station manager that there was trouble in paradise. The sprinklers that went off in his office did that for us. They also went off in the booth, just as I announced a 90 percent chance of sunshine.

My pride survived. The suit was history. It was the one thing I had bought right in my college career. No polyester imitations here, this was the real wool McCoy. The dry cleaner looked at it that afternoon, tinged with smoke and running with water, and laughed so hard he had to leave the counter.

So the next day I faced the most important interview of my life in khakis. And I didn't get the job. Instead, I ended up doing a ten-month stint as weekend sports man in a town so small I gave Little League scores on Saturday night.

Working there I had plenty of time for other things, like plotting revenge. Mighty Casey himself, the day after, didn't get more detailed.

And last week, after nearly five years, I got my chance. Normally, sitting at the newspaper sports desk is the last thing I will do. However, I had made a desperate trade of time at the desk in exchange for a couple of basketball tickets for my night off.

While I sat there, my victim delivered herself gift-wrapped into my hands. Should I be faulted if, when I discovered she was looking for Bat Masterson, I directed her to him in less than perfect circumstances? And I had to make sure the moment was captured on film.

Is revenge sweet? Let's just say there's joy in Mudville. Oh, and you people who sat outside that window and laughed like hyenas? I've got your names, at least the seven in the front row. You're next.

_____ TWO _____

Meg would have thought Monday morning was terrible if she hadn't had Friday for comparison. Compared to Friday in the locker room, Monday morning was only mildly awful. It was almost lunchtime when she got to her own safe desk. It looked like a haven, especially with Kim Harris and Dr. Liz Peters perched on each corner like bizarre bookends.

Her two friends couldn't have been more different. Kim, short and dark, with skin the color of café au lait and short curly hair, one leg swinging in nurse's white. Liz, pale and tall and angular, with straight black hair accentuating her pale skin, elegant even in blue surgical scrubs. And both of them looked more welcome than anything Meg had seen since that stupid locker room.

Kim, with a ready smile that lit her face and sparkled in her deep brown eyes, would have a way to put this all into perspective. When she saw Meg, she slid down from the desk. "So, do you need any boxes? I know where there's some dandies out by the loading dock."

Meg smiled weakly. "No thanks, Kim. I still have a job, just barely. But an hour in with Harbison is still pretty brutal."

Liz reached out a long arm and turned her around, surveying her from all angles. "An hour, huh? After what he had to say, I bet you're lucky to still have skin. Looks like you're intact, though." She gave her a quick hug, then let her go with a rueful smile. "You have to admit, the pictures are priceless."

Meg grimaced and sat down heavily in her desk chair, the other women still on either side of her desk. Several staffers had cut pictures out of their weekend newspapers. Spread on the desktop, the pictures were all versions of the same thing: a wide-eyed Meg, cheeks puffed out, flattened against the door to the whirlpool room.

"I've still got a friend from college who works for the Associated Press," Meg said, toying with the corner of one scrap of newsprint. "She called to tell me that one paper she saw ran a double shot, one of this one and one taken about a minute later of me kicking the wall and ripping down Alex's note. She's mailing me one for my scrapbook."

"Are you on probation or anything, or can you be seen in the cafeteria? I'll buy you lunch if you want," Kim offered.

"Let's bypass the cafeteria. I don't want to answer any more questions about Masterson's trunks, or lack of them, or Alex Langdon, or anything else."

"But you're okay?" Liz questioned, blue eyes serious.

"I'll survive," Meg said, trying not to sound shaky.

"All right," Liz said. "I've got to get back upstairs before my beeper goes off. Make sure she eats," she ordered Kim.

"I will," Kim promised Liz's retreating figure. Meg reached under her desk for her purse.

"When you said you knew somebody in TV sports, I didn't know you knew the hottest media personality in town," Kim said. "He's a hunk."

"True. He's also conceited, cocky, pushy. . . ." Meg paused to find just the right words to add to the list. "Before I went in with Harbison, I was ready to kill Alex. But then Harbison said he was ready to fire me until he read the column. And I *do* still have a job."

"But if Alex hadn't gotten involved in the first place, none of this would have happened," Kim said as they stood waiting for the elevator.

"None of it would have made it on film, anyway. I'm not so sure I wouldn't have done something equally stupid on my own," Meg said. "It's the major reason I haven't started making funeral plans for Langdon yet."

The other reasons were pretty good, too. In her heart Meg admitted she deserved the reception she got Friday. Alex, of all people, had the right to do something like this. That little stunt with his copy the morning after that fraternity party had earned her this, even five years later.

Granted, she'd gotten up feeling like a woman scorned that morning, but setting fire to his copy was one of those moments she wished she could undo as soon as it was done. Alex never gave her the chance. In one flick of flame they'd gone from being . . . Meg was stumped for a way to define their relationship. Friends didn't say enough; lovers wasn't accurate. And obviously, as much as she'd hoped for it, lovers had never been part of the agenda for Alex. He'd made that painfully clear that night, and ever since.

No time for reminiscing, she reminded herself. Now she was going to have lunch with Kim and forget the deep hole she'd dug for herself. After lunch she could worry about placating her boss, getting Gabe connected with Masterson, and facing the inevitable meeting with Alex. Well, at least after lunch she'd worry about her boss and Gabe. Meeting Alex was going to take more planning than just one afternoon.

Forty-five minutes of Kim, sunshine, and sweet and sour pork put Meg in an expansive mood. The sunshine in the little courtyard of the hospital was just what she needed to put everything in perspective. When Kim went back to work, Meg sat for a few more minutes before she gathered up the cartons and tossed them into the trash. There was a newspaper on one of the tables and she turned to Alex's column, deftly bypassing the pictures on the front of the sports section.

She read the column again. It had been a surprise, even after she knew Alex had set her up in the locker room. "Spotted imp from hell," indeed. As if he were a bargain as a sponsor, or anything else. And blaming her for his not getting that sports job in Indianapolis was arrogance she would have thought was beyond even Alex. Did he really think at twenty-two, with no other experience than campus radio, that he was ready for that?

She thought back to Alex at twenty-two, golden, charming, and magnificently insolent. Yes, he would think that, even now. Meg shook her head. Even with all this, she couldn't hate him. She was almost ready to laugh at Alex Langdon and his evil joke when the elevator opened on her floor.

A large green vase stood on her desk. Someone had sent her flowers while she was at lunch. Maybe she'd misjudged Alex after all. The flowers had to be from him. Crossing the room, she had visions of a wonderful note from him, full of unique eloquence in the form of apologies. Those ended when she got about three feet from the desk.

Alex had sent her flowers, all right. A dozen of the blackest, deadest roses she'd ever seen drooped from lank olive-green stems. A frayed once-white ribbon was tied around the vase, and a card hung from it. Meg yanked it off the ribbon to read the message. The move sent crisp brown and black petals cascading to her desk. "Nice, Langdon, real nice," she muttered.

The message was brief. "Now we're even. Alex." Meg looked at her watch. So maybe she wouldn't placate her boss or get Gabe his meeting this afternoon. Alex had suddenly moved himself up to top priority, ready or not. But after the chewing out she'd gotten from Harbison this morning, she had to stay for a while, even if her mind was going to be somewhere else. She had two hours to simmer until she could leave the hospital and go to a certain television station. The roses left a trail of crunchy little petals all the way to the dumpster.

You're not going to make a scene in the lobby, Meg told herself, looking at the marble walls and the receptionist's knowing smile. She watched the young woman punch the buttons on the interbuilding phone that called Alex. There was no sense turning into a screeching harridan in a public place, even though she'd feel better.

More than once, she'd fantasized meeting him again after five years. The fantasies were always great. They had nothing to do with wanting to curl her fingers around his massive neck and squeeze. However, life seldom imitates fantasy, and Alex, Meg told herself while she waited for him, never imitated anything.

She would be nice if it killed her. After all, she couldn't kill him. It would take an elephant gun. So she'd have to settle for a confrontation that would leave them both alive.

"You're late," Alex said without preamble when he came through the door. "I expected you at least two hours ago."

"Couldn't leave work," Meg said, forcing a swallow. The image of Alex had followed her for five years, but it had been a safe image on paper, or a screen, or tucked away in her memory. It didn't have the impact of six foot, two inches of real Alex. There he was at a distance their outstretched arms could have bridged. Looking at him, even from the front, sent a wave of recognition through her. "Now why didn't I know right away that cameraman in the goofy cap was you, even from that angle?"

He smiled and the lights in the broad marble lobby seemed to go out in comparison. Meg felt her intake of breath. "Yeah, that was me," he admitted. "I couldn't resist. I couldn't set up something that good and not watch."

The receptionist was openly watching the two of them, making no pretense of even trying to answer the phones. Alex tapped her gently on the shoulder. "Hello. Station KTIX . . ." he prompted, leaning low and speaking softly in her ear.

"Oh, yeah." She punched a button and made a halfhearted effort to go back to work.

"Let's not stand out here in the lobby. I have an office, sort of. Why don't we go back there?"

"Fine," Meg said, trying to stay as far away as possible. That worked great until the doorway. Alex's holding a door open crowded the opening severely. She had to squeeze past him, nearly touching.

He wore a spicy, sharp cologne she hadn't smelled before, but it suited him. She noticed idly that he'd discarded his tie some time during the afternoon and the top two buttons of his shirt were open, leaving dark blond chest hair to curl out, teasingly, just at her eye level.

Even as mad as she was at him, Meg's fingers

itched to trace that dark gold path. That was one part of things with Alex she'd hoped would be different. Here, in touching range, she knew with certainty that it would never be different. She'd always want to pick up just where she left off with Alex's body.

"We're standing in the doorway, Mutt," he said softly.

She pushed past him. "Meg. Margaret. Even Mary Margaret, which I detest, would be better than Mutt, Alex. I didn't even like it six years ago, when you answered to Jeff. Why do you think I'd like it now?"

"It just slips out automatically. M. Margaret Shepherd is way too much name for a little twerp like you. I noticed you didn't ever get that late growth spurt you always told me was going to happen," he said behind her. Even without turning, Meg could feel the sparkle to his eyes as he teased her. She could also feel his eyes on her back, which made it hard to walk the straight line of the burgundy carpeted hall.

"Let's stop harping on the size thing, okay? I get along just fine with most of the world," Meg said.

"I'll bet you do. How do they keep from mistaking you for one of the patients over there at the kiddie hospital, Mu . . . Mary Margaret?"

"Easy. They wear pajamas, or those funny-looking things that are open up the back. Besides, Alex, most of them are real sick. I may still look like a teenager sometimes, but I look like a healthy teenager."

"Without a doubt," Alex said with an inflection that made Meg's toes curl in her pumps.

The hall opened into a wide corridor with cubicles on either side. "Okay, now where am I going?"

Alex put a hand on her shoulder to steer, and Meg got a jolt. His hand was large and very warm through the fabric of her shirtwaist. It caressed her skin in such a way that she wished the fabric would just melt. Why couldn't she just stop moving and let his equally warm and solid body stop behind her? The thought had promise. She steered her mind back to Friday, remembering the expressions of the ball players in the whirlpool to try to fuel some outrage. It was hard to do with Alex's hand on her shoulder.

There had to be some reasons to keep a healthy dislike of Alex, Meg told herself. Let's see, what had she told Kim this morning? Conceited. Yes, Alex was certainly conceited. Of course, if you weren't in possession of a healthy self-confidence in his business, you didn't get anywhere. And most guys with his good looks would be conceited.

Cocky. Yep, that too. He still walked with the air of a man who had just won the lottery. The crisp striped shirt and tailored charcoal slacks just accentuated that walk, if anything could. Yes, Alex was still cocky.

Pushy still applied as well. Here he was, steering her down a hallway, in control as usual.

For the moment, though, Meg couldn't find a reason to object. The aura of sights and sounds and feelings that came rushing back the moment Alex touched her pushed all objections out of her mind.

Alex might be all those annoying things, but he was still Alex, too.

Funny, warm, goofy Alex. That was apparent the moment she walked into his cubicle. The inside walls of his office were made up of dividers. The nubby beige fabric was almost invisible. Every square inch was covered with pictures, cartoons, notes.

"Still easily bored, I see," Meg murmured, taking in the collection. There were several crazy cartoons of impossible dogs and a lot of twisted humor. Sports posters and ticket stubs from sports events took up their fair share of wall space, and the overflowing wastecan was crowned with an empty pizza box.

"I think it's almost time to move," Alex said behind her. "I've been in this one six months, and there's no more wall space left."

"True. You can hardly see the basketball hoop," Meg said, looking at the setup on one wall, hung from the top of one of the nubby dividers.

She could see Alex stretched out in his chair, sinking shots over the wastecan. That long, muscled arm would reach out, pump in a perfect two points, and go back to work in front of the PC effortlessly. The thought stirred a warmth in her. His shirt collar would pull open a little while he shot, and the momentary concentration would make his blue eyes flash. She had to keep reminding herself that she was mad at Alex, not mad about him. Meg forced a frown.

"Want a cup of coffee or something? Diet soda? A wooden stake to drive through my heart?" Alex's devilish smile dared her to say something.

"I'll pass on the stake. It wouldn't do any good," Meg said. "You don't have the required material to drive it through, Langdon."

"Me? Heartless?"

Meg whirled around. The innocent, baby-faced look she expected was there, widening Alex's eyes and rekindling her anger in earnest. "Heartless. For a practical joke you put me in a room full of naked baseball players, Langdon. And not only that, you set me up to be photographed on the way out. That wasn't funny. I nearly lost my job."

"Aw, not really. Your boss, what's-his-name, Harmon, or whatever, he's decent enough. . . ."

"Harbison," Meg said, the anger draining out of her flushed face, replaced with shock. "Alex, you talked to him?"

"Sure, called him this morning, just to make sure you weren't in too deep. Fun's fun, but I don't want you unemployed. You might sue me or something. And I've got to disagree about the pictures. They're a scream, especially the one with your cheeks pooched out like a chipmunk's." He closed his eyes and laughed softly, and Meg thought about pounding her fist into his chest. Only the knowledge of what the impact would do to her fragile self-control stopped her.

"That's juvenile. This whole practical joke thing is. Let's end it here, okay?"

"Is that what you came over here for? To ask me to leave off practical jokes. You're about five years too late, aren't you, Mutt?"

"Yeah, but whose fault is that? I would have

ended it there if you would have let me, Alex.
You're the one who wouldn't speak to me, not for
weeks.''

Alex shook his head. "Those little halfhearted
petty attempts weren't apologies. Not the kind I
wanted. You could have done better.''

Meg remembered her one attempt at doing better
and the reception that it got. If Alex wanted to talk
about small and petty, that was a good place to start.
Still, that was years ago, and this was now. Life
goes on. Maybe she would believe it if she said it
out loud. "We're adults now, Alex. The jokes have
to stop. I got your lovely bouquet, and you say we're
even now. Well, if we're even like you say, I want
to start without all that college stuff again. Is that
possible?''

He stepped very close to her, and Meg felt the
pulse in her throat and temples quicken with the nearness of him. "Possible, but not real probable, Mutt.
Look me in the eye and tell me you can forget
everything.''

His chest was so tempting this close. Meg wanted
to tell him that she'd forgotten. But she hadn't. Especially not that feeling that always came with Alex
less than three feet from her. It was coming now, in
waves about to engulf her. Her mouth was dry, and
Meg found her answer would only come with effort.
"I guess not. But can we call a truce? And can I
have that soda?''

Alex stepped back. "Sure. Machine's down the
hall. I'll be right back.''

The cubicle was much cooler without Alex in it.

Meg looked around at the clutter on the shelflike desk. Two local Emmys, tossed in a corner, were thick with dust. Best sports reporting, best sports feature, and Alex didn't even keep them shiny. That was normal. For Alex it was the chase that was the thrill, not the capture.

Meg bent to look at two photos in little magnetic frames on the file cabinet. One was of Alex, tanned and smiling, with an arm draped around a woman Meg had never seen. Meg stiffened when she looked closer. This was that woman.

Meg still had the card, tucked away with all those other impossible little mementos in her pack rat box. She didn't ever haul it out to look at. That would be too painful.

Still, Meg kept it. One of those ostentatious foil Christmas cards with the heavy envelopes. On the inside was an embossed preprinted signature. Mr. and Mrs. Alex Langdon.

When it had come, three years ago, she'd dropped it like a snake on the rug. It wasn't what she expected. Not after writing pages to Alex telling him how sorry she was for the way things had turned out. How she wished she'd gone to his graduation, and he to hers. How she still wanted, desperately, to be friends again. To start over.

An empty card with a preprinted signature. That was the only response she had gotten. But it had been enough to tell her what she needed to know.

Meg looked at the picture again in slightly ill fascination. She looked at the two people, their shiny gold wedding bands evident. According to her old college roommate, Cindi, they hadn't stayed shiny long.

In the picture, Alex was smiling, but he didn't look happy. There was a tightness to the smile that made Meg want to reach into the frame and massage his temples. The woman with him in the picture surely wouldn't. Not with talons like that. She'd chip her blood-red polish if she ever tried. Everything about her had the air of being too carefully tended, almost untouchable. Meg wondered how long she'd endured the arm around her shoulders after the shot was snapped.

Her sleek aqua swimsuit had never seen water, surely. Meg could envision what had happened on the beach in the background, later in the afternoon when Alex came charging out of the water, white trunks dripping, droplets falling out of his hair, made curly by the water. Meg could hear the shriek of outrage that would come from such a woman if a wet, exhilarated Alex tried to scoop her up from her shaded refuge. Her paperback would get all wet, and the pristine terry wrap might get sand on it.

Alex was quiet for a large man. Meg jumped when he spoke right behind her. "Ah, I see you found the honeymoon photo."

"Sure did."

Alex's intonation was flat. "When I didn't make a network sports anchor in the eleven months I knew Trudi, she decided we had irreconcilable differences. Most expensive differences I've ever seen."

"I'm sorry," Meg said, popping open her soda

can so that she didn't have to look into his eyes anymore and see the darkening hurt there.

"Sorry I was married, or sorry I'm divorced?"

"Both," she admitted, listening to his bark of laughter. "I would always wish you happiness, Alex. But . . . Trudi there doesn't look like she made you very happy."

Alex sat in the straight chair he'd pulled from a corner, turning it backward and straddling it in one fluid motion while Meg sat in his chair on wheels. "Let's just say it was an educational experience." There was a hardness in his eyes Meg didn't like seeing. Alex had always been canny but never bitter. She hated thinking of him that way now.

She took another drink of the cold liquid and turned back to the file cabinet. "What happened to the rest of the pictures?"

"Trudi kept the album. What I had, I burned. I just kept that one to bring me back to reality if I start waxing poetic about any female again."

"That one? But I saw two . . ." Meg started as she looked back to the frame. "Oh."

The other picture was not Trudi. Looking at it, she felt herself stretching back in time. The other picture was two people, really smiling, laughing out loud. They were wet and paint spattered, and there were no tension lines in Alex's face. Instead he stood, leaning forward over an old metal bedstead as a younger version of her own face looked back at her.

She remembered that day, the fraternity-sponsored races where teams of men had pushed the rickety old beds on wheels around a track, dodging obstacles of all kinds while their female navigators tried not to fall off. Victory had been hilarious, and just as the camera had flashed, Alex had said something rude.

So there she was, her eyes nearly crinkled shut, freckles everywhere, hair flying. She could still feel the hardness of Alex's chest when she'd flung her head back laughing, listening to him laugh. "Why did you hang on to this all this time?" she asked softly.

"It keeps me from burning the other one," he said curtly and stood up. "I look at it when I'm ready to give up on the human race. It reminds me I am capable of being truly happy."

Meg couldn't look at him for a while after that. Truly happy? That had been the day before she'd set fire to his news copy, the day before she'd gotten so miserably drunk . . . she knew he was probably thinking of it, too.

The pain seeped back in with the memories. She stared at the floor while she spoke. "You never spoke to me again, Alex, not a civil word for nearly five solid years. I wrote, I called, I walked up to you in hallways. Dammit, Alex, I nearly flunked out that semester."

"Just from worrying about me?"

"No, dummy, you had all my notes for three classes."

"I returned those," Alex argued.

"Oh? When?"

"That great big manila envelope I shoved under your door."

"Alex, that was confetti."

"Okay, so maybe I got a little enthusiastic removing the notes from the notebooks," Alex said, tilting his chair onto two legs for a moment.

"And really, Langdon, I didn't know it was your only suit, not until this morning. If I had . . ."

"Your daddy would have provided me with a new one, right?" Alex said. There was a flash of disdain in his look that made Meg's temper flare.

"No. I would have. Don't you start that again."

"Start what again?"

"The class stuff. So my parents helped me through school. Stop making me feel like a spoiled rich brat for that, all right?" She was up out of her chair before she even thought about it, facing him.

"All right, already. Get off your high horse. Still, you did have it easier."

"Different, Alex. Not easier. I still had to work for everything I got. My parents may have paid my way, but I was there on partial scholarship, remember? One B minus and my scholarship would have gone straight out the window."

Alex's smile was wolfish. "I know. Why do you think I always borrowed your notes? I knew they'd be better than mine."

"I give up." Meg swung a mock cuff at him, just swiping his crisp, dark honey hair. She looked closer at it. "You're going gray."

"Impossible. That's just sun bleaching."

"It's hardly even April, Alex. You're going gray."

"Sun. I was in Mexico a month ago on a cruise."

"Alone?"

"Of course not. I had twenty-five rabid baseball fans along, and three players. It was a blast." His enthusiasm sounded hollow.

Meg ruffled his hair, unable to keep from touching it. She wanted to do more, but this wouldn't invade his precious privacy. His hair was wonderfully textured. "I still say it's gray."

His reflexes hadn't gone. Before she could back away from the chair, Alex had wrapped his arms around her in a grip that was stunning. "It. Is. Sun. I'm too young for gray. Got it?"

"Got it," Meg said, cursing the breathy quality of her own voice. Her chin was less than inches from that magnificent head of hair now, and she could smell the expensive shampoo he used. The scent matched his cologne, warm waves of spicy sharpness rising in the heat of him.

For a moment, feeling his hands on her back and the hard metal of the chair pressed into her ribs, Meg fought the urge to touch him again. But the need was stronger than anything else, and she buried her face in his hair. Her arms twined around his shoulders, broad and smooth, muscles rippling under the cotton of his shirt.

There was an inarticulate sound from Alex and his hands pulled her even closer to him, roaming across her shoulder blades, then traveling down over her body to draw her to him. It was a delicious feeling, but only half as wonderful as the feel of him under her fingertips. Meg found one hand moving up, into the nape of his neck, into that dark gold tangle of hair there, the sweetest of spots.

Alex made that sound again, but this time it was muffled as he nuzzled into the open collar of her shirtwaist. Meg felt a rivulet of shock, hot and tingly, moving down to the pit of her stomach. Where had those top three buttons gone all of a sudden, the traitors?

There had been a few men in her life since college. They were mostly quiet, pleasant fellows from the hospital or brothers of someone who thought she needed to go out more. Two of them had even kissed her, and Meg still remembered each kiss. All the feelings she had felt during both of those kisses could have been put in the space between Alex's lips and her breastbone in the first three seconds of contact. And there would have been feelings left over, feelings that Alex was stirring up quite vividly with his expressive mouth against her skin.

When Meg felt herself surge against his lips, her entire body moving upward and into his embrace, for a moment she was rocketed back in time. But she wasn't going back in time; she was solidly in the here and now. So was Alex. His thighs bracketed her, keeping her close to him and the chair.

She was suddenly very aware that this cubicle had no door and Alex had no reason to be holding her like this.

"Alex," she said, letting her fingers slide over his shoulder blades, down his arms, reaching the cold metal of the chair.

He groaned and rested his forehead against her

collarbone. "Oh, no. We're doing it again, aren't we, Mutt?"

"Meg. Maggie, even. Anything, Alex. And yes, we are. What are we going to do about it?"

His eyes were clear dark blue. "Do we have to do anything about it?"

Meg snapped to attention. A rush of anger pulled her out of his arms. "Of course we do. It's just hormones, Langdon. Somewhere there's some crazy hormone call between you and me that kicks in every time we're alone." That had to be the only explanation. She knew it was for Alex, and it had to be for her. There was a bitter taste on her tongue at the thought of being involved with Alex again and the wanting that would engender. It made moving away from him much easier.

"This hormone thing. It bothers you?" His voice was languorous, and he smiled as he leaned his chin against his crossed arms on the back of the chair.

Obviously, he couldn't see the trembling that was going on. "Of course it bothers me. This doesn't happen with any of my other friends."

"So I'm back to friend status?"

Meg tried to be casual as she buttoned her buttons again. Sirens were screaming in her head at the thought of being friends with Alex. "I guess so."

"Good thing, since we'll be seeing so much of each other."

"What are you talking about? We haven't seen each other in five years, and if you hadn't sent me a bunch of dead roses . . ."

"Now I thought that was just the right touch."

"Charming, Langdon, just charming. Anyway, If you hadn't sent those, we wouldn't be seeing each other now."

"And here I thought it was my magnetic charm, Mutt. I thought you just couldn't stay away any longer."

"Don't you just wish," Meg said, wishing her voice wasn't still trembling a little.

"Maybe I do. Anyway, you'll be back. You see, I have something you need," Alex said, looking incredibly smug as he stood up.

"Nothing you have is anything I need that badly, Alex," Meg said, picking up her purse. "How about leading me out of this maze?"

"Sure. Might as well memorize it. You'll be back."

"Don't hold your breath," Meg muttered. "You might turn purple."

"Not a chance." His voice was smug. "A compassionate woman like you would give me CPR first. And then we'd be right back where we started."

"We already are," Meg said smoothly as she walked through the door. She congratulated herself for being cool and collected in front of the smirking receptionist.

She hadn't counted on Alex and his love of the last word, or lack of words. The hand on the small of her back was firm and swift, and the kiss that followed as he bent her backward in a classic move was as quick and devastating as a fire storm.

Meg wasn't sure whether the hands she put on his chest were pushing him away or just clinging for support. She was back on her feet, watching the door swing closed behind him, before she could say anything.

"Don't ask," she told the gaping woman with the headset dangling from one ear, a bank of buzzing phones in front of her. "Don't even ask."

THE MORNING STAR   SECTION D
             COMMENTARY
             Alex Langdon

The tempest in a teacup or, rather, a whirlpool, after Friday's game has stirred up another controversy. Or re-stirred up a very old controversy. Where were you people three years ago, anyway? Every baseball fan in the city couldn't have spent that much time under a rock.

For all of you who've called and written, you're right. My dear friend Mutt Shepherd would have been spared a lot of grief if she'd known what all of you do. Michael "Bat" Masterson does not speak to the press. No reporters, no public relations people, no nothing. And that is his prerogative.

He is not just being a difficult star. Mike Masterson stopped speaking to the press when he was a talented rookie. And apparently very few people remember why.

I remember why, because I was there when it happened. As a visiting reporter with the "away" team, I took a busman's holiday to check out the other guy's hot rookie.

So I stood in a suburban mall watching Masterson sign autographs. The other folks there have apparently chosen to forget the incident in their pique over the fact that Masterson won't talk to them anymore. Of course, if I were he, I wouldn't talk to them either. Heck, even not being him, I still don't talk to many of them.

Mike Masterson doesn't talk to the press because he doesn't have anything to say to them. He had something to say when he came up to the majors, but very few people asked him. Once he started pitching a tremendous amount of winning games, and at the same time batting in a surprising number of game-winning runs, suddenly everyone realized he might have something to say.

So they started talking to Masterson. He was a friendly, outgoing kid from Union, with no grudges against anybody. He still is, but he's gotten a little wiser.

The wisdom is mostly from life experience. In the first wave of success, the team asked Masterson to do promotional stuff. He went to shopping centers, sporting goods stores, other public places and signed autographs. He talked to

Little League players and their parents, and he made a lot of friends.

Most members of the press weren't counted among those friends. Let's face it, a nice kid from a small town who plays good ball and goes to sporting goods stores to talk to nine-year-olds is boring. Nobody much had the time in thirty-second sound bites to dig deep enough for the charisma, so they didn't find it.

Mike Masterson just kept on being nice and being boring until that day at the mall. There was a huge crowd, as usual. One large family had several tow-headed little kids, cute little suckers with "photo opportunity" nearly stamped on their foreheads. When they all clustered around Masterson, flashes started going off. Mama and Daddy were so busy watching the older guys get Masterson's autograph that they didn't notice the littlest sprout, who decided to go investigate the escalator.

Suddenly there were noises from the crowd as everyone at once saw this kid throw his chubby little leg over the side of the escalator handrail. The floor on the other side of the railing was two stories below.

Masterson has wonderful reflexes. He dropped his pen, sprinted the 20 feet or so, and picked up the kid before anybody else thought about it. The flashes went off again. They kept going off when he hugged the little guy, a pint-sized fellow in a mock uniform. They continued to go off when the little guy got real excited and did what excited little guys sometimes do, all over Masterson's shirt.

Masterson's reaction this time was equally swift and natural. The kid wasn't caused any pain, but no time was wasted in removing him from Masterson's presence. There was a little laughter, and the autograph session petered out.

Walking to my car, I found Masterson. "That's the shot they're all going to use," I told him. "Not the catch, the reaction." He looked at me like I was crazy.

No, he told me, that wouldn't happen. The sportswriters respected him and the team. There were plenty of other things to talk about without embarrassing him and the poor little kid.

Have it your way, I told him, until the morning paper comes out. But that's the shot they're going to use.

Of course they did. Sports fans all over the Midwest were treated to the sight of Masterson, a look of real disgust on his face, holding a squalling toddler at arm's length. There was no attempt to explain what really went on, and the angle of the pictures covered the incriminating spots pretty well.

That was the last public appearance Masterson ever bothered with. It suddenly dawned on him that he hadn't lost anything that could be found in shopping malls, or sporting goods stores, or in the company of newspaper and television reporters. So he just doesn't talk.

At least, he doesn't talk for publication. He still talks, to a few people. Actually, he still talks to me. If I printed one word of what he said, he'd stop that, too. So I don't print it or spout it on the evening news.

Because Mike Masterson is still a nice guy. He's still a man whose perceptions come from a small town, where folks didn't lock their doors at night and playing baseball was every kid's dream. He grew up to fulfill that dream, even if it's a little ragged around the edges. I listen to Mike Masterson because he's got something to say worth hearing. It's just a shame that nobody else gets to hear it.

THREE

"Damn, damn, and double damn." Meg, at her desk, nearly threw her coffee cup against a wall. She crumpled the newspaper in front of her to hide the smug face in the picture next to the byline. So Alex Langdon was the only one who talked to Mike Masterson. The self-satisfied look on his face after he had kissed her yesterday made perfect sense now.

Of course, he expected her to come back. Masterson didn't answer telephone calls or return messages. Meg could just imagine what writing him would accomplish, and she knew she'd never get another chance at a personal appointment with him on her own. Just the thought of what had happened the last time still made her blush from her shoulder blades on up.

Maybe it wasn't as important to Gabe as she thought it was. Maybe she'd go down to his room and find out how he was doing. Meg smiled. It couldn't be as bad as she was imagining. There had to be plenty of ways to keep half a city between herself and Alex. She put the lid back on her cache of chocolate-covered raisins, snitching one for the trip to Gabe's room.

No one in the elevator made any snide jokes about baseball players, a fact that Meg was thankful for. Perhaps things were finally going to cool down on that front. She stepped out onto the third floor and went past the nurses' station, an unspoken question in the tilt of her head.

Kim Harris was there, looking serious. "He's in there. And, Meg, it's not so great today."

Meg's buoyed-up spirits sank even before she got to Gabe's door. It was quiet in his room, no raucous music playing, no friends sitting on his bed. That was a bad sign. So was his pallor when she pushed open the door and went in.

Gabe was half propped on a pillow, and Meg was shocked by the clarity with which she could see all the bones at his wrist, stretched out on top of the blanket. His shock of yellow hair was uncombed and his eyes were dull. His father, Spence, sat next to him. Normally, Meg found the older farmer's solid nature, his square hands and silvering crew cut, comforting. Today he and his son were both just very quiet.

Spence looked up when Meg entered the room and forced a faint smile. "Well, Gabe, here's Ms. Shepherd come to see you. You can tell her hello, can't you?"

" 'Lo.'' Gabe's eyes seemed to be focused, unmoving, at a point about two feet past the foot of the bed.

Meg stood by the bed, inhaling the smell of antiseptic and cleaning solutions. "Hey, sport. What's happening? Don't tell me the skin graft they did is failing?"

"Nope. It's fine. Itches like . . . anything," he said, editing his language for her. Meg smiled a little. Whatever was happening, it couldn't be terminal. When Gabe still had his manners, he would come around.

"Then what's going on?"

"We got a letter from the county school board. Now they're saying he may not be able to graduate with his class."

"Oh, no." It was one of the things that kept Gabe hanging on. The teenagers who came by the carload every two or three weeks kept him current on the social scene, and his mother and father brought him homework by the sheaf. "Why not?"

"They're not sure he's really keeping up even though the homework is getting done," Spence said. His expression let Meg know exactly what he thought of the school board's opinions. "They want him to take some kind of standardized tests to prove he's really at grade level."

"That's no problem," Meg said. "We can clear the dayroom at the end of the hall and set up a testing area. They can send whomever they like. We can't have them flunking Gabe. A battalion of nurses would storm their board meeting."

Gabe smiled at the thought. "Yeah, Kim would

probably lead the charge.'' The smile faded quickly.
"I'm not sure, though, Meg. I really need some
work on math. I might flunk their test.''

"How much time have we got?"

"No later than May first," Spence said. "Why?"

"We could arrange for a tutor. I can do some
calling to St. Louis city and county schools and see
what we can work out," Meg said.

"That's very kind of you, Meg. Can we go down
the hall to talk for a minute? I think Gabriel needs
a rest.''

Gabe snorted. "Right, Dad. At ten in the morning? Just go talk to Meg in private.''

Meg felt sympathy for him, stretched out under
the white sheets. "We'll be back.''

They went down the hall and turned the corner,
standing by a bank of tall windows. Spence looked
out, not seeing the traffic below. "We appreciate the
offer to hunt up a tutor, Meg. But we can't. We
can't even afford the hospital right now, much less
money for a tutor. It'd just kill him, though, to miss
graduating with his class. I'm stuck on this one.''

Meg had never seen Spence at a loss before. And
she'd seen a lot of him. He and Martha split the
visiting. Spence came in the daytime whenever the
farm didn't keep him there. Martha came in the eve-
nings once she got off from the office job in Washington, Missouri, that provided the hospitalization
that was paying for her son's expensive treatment
when the farm couldn't.

Even in the worst of it, two months before, when
Gabe had been in intensive care and his parents had

taken turns sleeping in the tiny chapel nearby, Spence had fought like a tiger for his son. Now he looked lost. She crossed the distance and hugged him hard.

He hugged her back, the metal buttons of his denim jacket pressing into her as she gave him a pep talk. "You stop worrying about this. Let's use our energy to get Gabe well. And forget about the money for a tutor. I'll find somebody who'll work for free if I have to, or do some arm twisting."

Spence drew back. "That's too much. We can't ask you to do any more for him. You have a whole hospital full of patients to answer for and other things to do. You can't keep spending your time looking out for Gabe. First this baseball thing, now the tutor . . ."

Meg's spirits sagged. So much for Masterson not meaning much to Gabe.

Spence looked out the window. Meg could tell he didn't see the parking garage or the bright flowers that bordered it. "Dr. Liz says after this skin graft heals, all they have to do is make sure the bone has knit properly and start the physical therapy. We may only be here another month, or even less. But the therapy . . ." His voice caught, and Meg saw the constriction of his throat as he swallowed. "They said the therapy is going to be very painful for the first couple of weeks. I keep hoping Bat Masterson would see fit to talk to Gabe. It would help keep him going."

Meg was struck again by the single-minded concern that Spence showed for his son. "He doesn't say much, Meg, but he's so close to giving up at times. Dr. Liz says that a bad infection could undo everything again. If that happens, and he can't use the leg right again . . . well, I want to give him every chance we can.''

Suddenly calling Alex didn't sound so horrible after all. It sounded much less horrible than what Gabe was already going through. "I'll get right on the tutor,'' Meg promised. "And I've got a line on Masterson. But all the same, let's not tell Gabe anything yet, all right?''

"If I didn't tell him the day you got this idea, after that last surgery, I'm sure not going to tell him now,'' Spence said, running a hand over his iron-gray hair. "We'll wait until you're sure. I don't want to disappoint him.''

"We won't,'' Meg said. She wasn't sure how she was going to pull it off, but Bat Masterson would walk through Gabriel's hospital room door if she had to hog-tie him and put him on a gurney.

The lobby of the elegant downtown hotel was bright and airy, but even the four-story atrium wasn't containing Meg's soaring panic. What was she doing seeing Alex again, even in a public place like this? Surely there must have been some way to handle all of this by telephone. On the phone with Alex she just got snippy, and her palms sweat. That was far better than her reaction to him in person.

His voice was so smooth, even on the phone, that she had found herself inviting him to lunch before she realized what she was doing. At least she'd still had enough scraps of common sense left to suggest a very public, very businesslike place. The last time she'd had lunch here she'd been struck by the number of city officials and broker types sitting at the tables conducting business. And it would be nice to have a change of pace from salads with Kim in the hospital cafeteria.

Still, she wondered if she was doing the right thing. Catching her reflection in the glass wall next to her, she checked for little embarrassments, like swatches of lace slip and camisole straps. Neither peeked out, but she did question again the brilliance of wearing a black skirt this short in front of Alex.

Somehow, the image came to mind of waving a red flag in front of a bull. Meg could almost see him snorting and pawing the ground. She pushed the image away and looked out at the hurrying crowd on the sidewalk. Still no Alex. He was late, which was a rarity. Here she'd tried to match his old schedule and he was apparently adopting hers.

"Waiting for me?"

She knew it probably looked coy, but the hand pressed to her heart was not for effect. Alex's greeting made her jump, and turning around to look at him didn't bring down her pulse rate one bit. Alex was windblown, slipping dark sunglasses into the pocket of his suit jacket. On anybody else the combination of tailored attire on the top and pale, worn blue jeans on the bottom would have looked strange. On Alex it looked . . . huggable. No, she wasn't going to think about that. She was going to get him across this lobby, into the restaurant, and have a civilized, adult business luncheon. Her heart had slowed down a little, finally. "You love that, don't you, Langdon?"

"You do jump higher than anybody else I've ever seen. You almost got to shoulder height on me that time, Mutt."

"Very funny. Shall we have lunch?" Meg tried to sound frosty. It was hard to do, with Alex's warm grin melting her resolve. "I appreciate your taking time to meet me like this, Alex."

"It's the least I could do for an old friend." Something about the way he dragged out those last two words made Meg want to make faces at him, but she knew it wouldn't do any good. If she encouraged him he'd just get worse.

"No, the least you could have done was wear all of your suit. Haven't you gotten tired of playing rebel that way?"

Alex shrugged. "Nobody sees the jeans when I'm on the air, and nobody cares otherwise. I might as well be comfortable. You should have seen me in the ice storm last winter, with my wool socks and boots."

"I'm sure it was just charming. . . ." Meg trailed off in midsentence. The hotel had redecorated the restaurant since she'd been here. The glass and chrome and slick black and red decor were gone. Instead everything was about as businesslike as a Venetian bordello. The lighting was dim, and everything was done in gray, lavender, and mauve. Candle sconces and lots of crystal prisms and gold florets were everywhere. Meg swallowed hard, standing next to the heavy antique sideboard that obviously served as the maître d's station.

The man swooped down on the two and seated them in one of the plush side booths before Meg had a chance to protest. Alex was sitting much closer to her side of the semicircular seat than she would have liked while he perused the menu.

"Let's see. Oysters Rockefeller, angel hair pasta with shrimp and cream . . . who's paying for this shindig, Mutt, you or the hospital?"

"It depends. You involved in the charity ball your station is throwing for our cancer research fund?"

"Not yet."

"You want to be?"

"What do I have to do? I warn you, I'm a lousy emcee. And the auctions that sell off bachelors have never been able to get rid of me, not since that first year when I . . . well, anyway, I'm not a good auction item."

"You're joking," Meg said, looking up from her menu. "I would have thought you'd bring premium price, as good-looking as you are."

"No, I think the predate agreement I have the ladies sign puts a damper on my bidding. Did you really mean it?"

"What? About the hospital paying? As long as I could agree to get you to come to the charity ball, and mingle a little, this is business. . . ."

"I can do that," he said impatiently. "I meant the other part. You think I'm good-looking?"

"Come on, Langdon, your vain mug leers out from every newspaper in town, and you've got the highest Nielsen ratings of any sportscaster in the metro area. They don't pay you to be ugly."

"Yes, but you always used to say my nose was too big." He genuinely looked as if he believed it.

"Did I? I don't remember that." Meg moved her head to one side, studying him. "It's nicely shaped, anyhow, even if there is plenty of it."

"And you know what they always say about nose size," Alex said, grinning.

Meg was mystified. "No, I don't."

Alex lost half of his grin, so that only one lopsided twinkle quirked a corner of his mouth. "I'd forgotten who I was talking to. No, you honestly wouldn't know."

For reasons she couldn't explain, Meg wanted to take off her suit jacket suddenly. No one else in the room seemed to be warm, but her temperature was rising. However, sitting next to Alex in the cream-colored sleeveless shell she had on would be more uncomfortable than the warmth she felt.

"Will you be ordering for the lady, sir?" The waiter had apparently been standing patiently for a while before either of them noticed him.

"No, I will not be ordering for the lady. Not on my life. The last time I ordered for the lady I was nearly skinned alive."

"It's passé, Alex. Besides, your tastes in food are revolting."

"Most people like schnitzel à la Holstein, Mutt. How was I supposed to know you wouldn't?"

"Alex, it had a fried egg on top of it. And the yolk was runny." Meg felt herself shudder just thinking about it. The waiter had a bemused look on his face, like someone watching the Marx brothers play tennis. This was beginning to be a habit among people listening to their conversations. She glanced at the menu again. "Chicken Caesar salad and a diet cola. Decaffeinated, if you have it."

Alex shook his head. "The woman won't eat a fried egg with a runny yolk, but totally raw eggs, that's okay."

"Alex, don't you start telling me what's in my lunch."

"All right, all right. Angel hair pasta and coffee. Real. Black."

The waiter nodded and left. Meg noticed that about ten feet from the table he looked at them over his shoulder once, just to see what they were doing. He must have been disappointed by the perfectly normal sight of Alex slipping off his suit coat and putting it on the seat next to him and Meg trying to get comfortable as far away from Alex as possible without falling off the end of the seat.

Meg hoped someone would come back soon with some bread or crackers or something. Not only was she hungry, but she needed a distraction from Alex's tanned throat below his tieless, open collar and the little gold glints in the hair on the back of his hands.

What she needed most of all was a distraction from the warm leg she was sure to encounter if she moved one fraction of an inch on the seat or stretched her feet out in front of her. This cozy booth was never meant for someone of Alex's lanky proportions unless he was with a very good friend.

Alex stretched himself even closer to Meg. "You didn't call me over here for lunch to ask me about a charity ball, did you, Mutt?"

"Meg. Margaret. Mary Margaret. Maggie." By the end of the litany, Alex was mouthing along, a feat that made her want to smack him in his all-too-perfect mouth. "And no, I didn't, Alex. You know that."

"Yeah, I do. What I don't know is why you wanted to talk to Masterson so bad. Are you really an ardent fan, like some of the other sportswriters suggested?"

Meg found herself getting warm again. "Of course not. I want him to come talk to one of our patients."

Alex shook his head and patted her hand. Where was that bread? "You're still taking in strays, aren't you? Tell me about the patient."

"His name is Gabe, and he's been in a little under nine weeks. He and his cousin were working on his dad's farm . . ."

"He's the kid who had the tractor fall on top of him," Alex said with a wince.

"Yeah, how'd you know?"

He looked abashed, if that was possible for Alex. "Once I found out you were working at the children's hospital, I guess I tended to read any news stories from there, just to see if they mentioned you. You do all right, you know."

Meg was oddly flattered. "Thank you. Anyway, Gabe is a baseball player, baseball fan, the whole works. And Masterson is his favorite player in the whole world. Alex, his entire wall is covered with pictures and statistics.''

"And naturally, he'd love for Masterson to come visit him with the cameras rolling, flashes popping . . .'' Alex sounded jaded.

"Not at all. He doesn't even know I'm trying to do this,'' Meg said, knowing her chin was stuck out stubbornly. She would have been able to feel sterner if she hadn't moved around on the seat. As it was, her leg was stretched out next to Alex's. She was electrically aware of the contact from her thigh to her ankle.

Alex looked as surprised as she felt. "He doesn't know?''

"Not a thing,'' Meg said, hoping she was still making sense. "We haven't told Gabe, because if Masterson won't come see him, nobody wants to disappoint him again. He's already been disappointed enough.'' Thinking about Gabe in that hospital bed made her forget for a little while the warm, welcoming length of Alex's leg against hers.

"He's missed just about all of his junior-year baseball season, Alex. He's going to turn seventeen in a hospital bed, not knowing if he's going to be able to walk right again, or ever play ball. And he's still at the point where one serious infection could probably be fatal.''

Alex looked at her as if he were gauging something. "And you think a visit from Masterson would mean that much to him?''

"Alex, I know Masterson's batting average from hanging around this kid. I know his ERA and what kind of glove he uses. Me, the sports illiterate of the century. Does that tell you something about Gabe and what a visit from Masterson would mean to him?''

''Yep.'' Alex's voice was soft, and his smile was almost sweet. ''It also tells me plenty about you. You haven't changed a bit, Mary Margaret Shepherd. You're still looking out for people and taking care of them. I'll bet you still bake four-layer chocolate cakes for people's birthdays, just like you did at the campus radio station.''

Did he realize he had reached over and was holding her hand? Surely he was just unconsciously doing that thing with his thumb over her palm. ''You were the only one who ever got a cake, Alex. Everybody else gets brownies.''

Before he could react, the waiter finally came back with their drinks and a basket of bread. Meg was thrilled to have a task that needed both hands, so that she had a reason to slip out of Alex's grasp.

Sitting this close to her, he could probably hear her stomach rumble. She knew what he could feel, if his nerve endings were as charged as hers by the close contact in this small space.

He could feel the warmth between them, the contrast of the smoothness of her hose to the texture of his worn jeans. Meg wondered if there was really that much static electricity between their legs or if they were creating their own charge out of something else.

Either way, it was good to have something to do that didn't involve touching Alex. Not that touching

Alex didn't feel good. It felt marvelous, but it wasn't likely to lead to anything except more touching Alex, and that would lead to trouble.

Alex was spreading a whole pat of butter on his bread, and he grinned when Meg wrinkled her nose. "What do you do to burn that off, Langdon? You don't look like you eat anything except sprouts and rice cakes."

"Perish the thought. I chase stories, mostly. Lunch is about the only solid meal I get some days. The rest of the time it's ballpark hot dogs, chips, peanuts, pizza somebody brings in the station . . ."

"I get the picture," Meg said, trying not to shudder. "Didn't you ever learn to cook?"

"No time, no inclination," Alex said. "I'd rather just eat something out of a can."

"Ugh. I remember that now. Those awful canned chili sandwiches . . ."

Meg was saved from remembering more of Alex's college concoctions when the waiter brought lunch. Alex was working on his second cup of coffee, and she'd almost forgotten their legs were stretched out together by the time the conversation started up again.

"So why're you at the hospital, anyway, Mutt? I always figured I'd turn on my television in some hotel on a road tour and there you'd be anchoring the news."

Meg looked at him. There was a twinkle in his blue eyes, but it was friendly, not malicious. "You honestly don't remember? My internship, the report from the fire . . ."

"Oh, yeah, that. I just figured you'd get over it."

"I never did. Never have." Never stopped freezing into a statue when the lights glared, never stopped feeling that her tongue was frozen when the camera was rolling on her. "I'm better off on the other side of the camera."

"So you do hospital PR." Alex shook his head.

"And do a darned good job at it, too, when nobody's directing me into locker rooms," she said, tilting her chin in a combative stance.

"I never said it wasn't a good job," Alex said, raising a palm in defense. "I just . . ." He trailed off, looking around. "Is that rain?"

Meg wondered how long there had been the steady drum on the windows without her realizing it. Watching Alex eat pasta had been distracting enough that she probably wouldn't have heard a cyclone. But now, there was the distinct thrum of a steady rain on the glass across the room.

"I hope I closed the sun roof," she said. "Do you mind if I go check?"

"As long as you don't stick me with the bill, you go right ahead," Alex said, leaning back in his seat and sipping his coffee.

She was back in a moment, having settled the bill on the way. "No damage. Baby's safe and secure."

Alex's eyebrows quirked. "Baby? Does this mean you're still naming your vehicles?"

"They have personality. You accepted enough rides in Clara, I recall, and didn't poke fun at her."

"Not that she deserved it or anything. That car was a horror."

"It got us places. But Baby is much better looking." Meg smiled. The sports car was her one little luxury.

"I'm going to have to ask you to prove it," Alex said, a rueful smile tilting one corner of his generous mouth. "I walked over here. It was such a nice day, and all . . ."

"And we can't have you ruin that suit coat, can we, Alex? You might throw me to the wolves again."

"Masterson and his crew are not wolves. Most of the time, anyway. But I would appreciate a ride."

"Come on, then," Meg said. "I'm parked right in front of the hotel. We can sprint."

Meg sprinted first, getting into the car quickly, sliding over to unlock his door. When Alex dashed from under cover of the awning and slid in next to her, Meg's eyes widened. The compact red car was just perfect for her. It was a cozy haven where she cocooned her way home every evening. Putting someone of Alex's height and breadth next to her redefined the space in a whole new way.

His slightly damp hair brushed the roof of the car as he settled into the seat. "This is yours?"

"Of course. Surprised?"

"Amazed. Leather seats and a CD?" His smile suddenly had a touch of grimness to it. "Sugar Daddy or just the regular one?"

"Neither," Meg said, trying to sound frosty. "I discovered I happen to like a few little luxuries."

"So you just marched out and bought yourself one."

"We all have our quirks. Throw something on for the ride if you want." Meg tried to sound nonchalant as she started the car and pulled out of the parking space in the steady rain that was still falling.

The car smelled of rain, and a damp warmth mixed with Alex's cologne. It didn't help her concentration any to have him rooting through the music. When a hand slid over onto her knee, she yelped and skidded to a stop at a changing light.

Alex removed his hand, with just the slightest squeeze of her knee. Even that little pressure sent shock waves up past her hip. "Sorry." He sounded almost sheepish. "I was trying to figure out how to get this in. The CD. And I wasn't looking where my other hand was going. Nice skirt."

"Thanks." Why wasn't the light changing?

"Nice hair, too. You always had the softest hair, Mutt." The music was throbbing in the background, and shivers skittered up Meg's neck as Alex traced a finger there. "You've got a little curl coming down, right here."

Now somebody else had a left turn. Meg closed her eyes, willing the light to turn green before she lost her sanity. Then the light really did change, and her hands and legs were all busy shifting into gear, moving forward at the same time that Alex got very busy himself.

The sound he made was almost a growl. It was

deep and very satisfied as he planted his lips at the spot where her neck sloped down to her shoulder. "Alex, I have to drive."

"Go right ahead. You're doing a great job of it." He always had a heavy beard, and even now, before two in the afternoon, it was rough against her skin. She imagined he kept a razor in his desk, and before he went on the air . . . The thought drove her almost as wild as what he was doing with her neck, and then her earlobe.

Putting out a hand only brought her in contact with his thigh, hard and muscular and unyielding. "Alex. Please."

"Please don't or please do? I nearly went crazy in that restaurant, Meg. Do you know you press your lips together every time you take a sip of anything?" His voice was husky in her ear, and it took every scrap of concentration to keep the car in her lane, then pull it to the curb in front of the television station.

It was still raining steadily. No one was on the street in front of the station. Perhaps that was why Alex didn't get out of the car right away. "Well, here we are." Meg tried to make it come out brightly, but her voice trembled.

"Yep, here we are," Alex said, smiling. He was still less than inches from her as he slid a hand up each side of her shoulders to caress her neck and frame her face. Before she could say anything, his mouth closed in on hers.

This time the kiss was no surprise, nor was her reaction to it. It was like coming home again after being away a long, long time. Alex's mouth slanted over hers as one hand buried in her hair. The heavy, aching sweetness of kissing him surrounded Meg as she wondered with the one part of her brain that was still functioning normally why it was never this way with anyone else.

Why did she get this surge of feeling, this powerful desire to melt into him, only with Alex? Why not with those perfectly nice young men she'd met in the last four years? Still kissing him, reveling in the sensation of his mouth, his searching tongue that lit fires, Meg felt a sob rising. When it threatened to break, she put both hands against his solid chest and firmly moved them apart.

Alex sat back in the seat, an unreadable expression on his attractive features. "Thanks for the lunch, Mutt. I'll try to see if Masterson would go for this."

"Please," Meg said, trying to keep her breathing even.

"I'll try. I can't make any promises. Remember, I'm the one who told him not to talk to anybody in the first place."

"All right."

Alex reached for the door handle. "Thanks for the ride over here." He broke into a smile. "Maybe we can finish it some other time." He tilted a finger under her chin and let it trail away as he opened the car door.

"In your dreams, Langdon. Only in your dreams." It sounded good, Meg thought, watching him sprint for cover, laughing. Now why couldn't she believe it?

THE MORNING STAR   SECTION D
COMMENTARY
Alex Langdon

"Only in your dreams." A friend said that to me recently. I think it was meant to be a putdown. But I sure like the sound of it. Only in your dreams.

I remember some of my dreams, the ones that started about the time I was nine. Those long summer days in Indiana seemed to stretch forever. During the daytime I did chores, aggravated my mother, biked to the municipal swimming pool, collected reptiles, and dreamed.

In my dreams I was the wickedest pitcher in the majors. After supper I would get a chance to make those dreams as close to reality as any nine-year-old ever does.

If there was no one to play ball with, I had one of those pale red rubber numbers I would take, along with my glove, and bounce against the steps leading down from the back porch.

Thwack. I can still remember the dull thumping sound that ball made when it hit the sun-bleached dusty porch step. It would carom off the wood, come up, and angle into my glove. Stance, pause, throw. Thwack, squint, catch. Sometimes it went on for hours.

The neighbors probably wondered about my intelligence. Of course, all they saw was a skinny kid in cutoff blue jeans, drooping T-shirt, tattered sneakers, and a baseball cap, throwing an old ball against the house.

They couldn't hear the roar of the crowd or see the catcher as he gave me the signals. I'll bet they couldn't smell the hot, dry dust of the infield or the peanuts from the stands. They probably couldn't even hear the music, those stupid little riffs for each batter, not even when I struck out Pete Rose.

Only in my dreams. My dreams were powerful things that brought to life an entire major league baseball stadium every evening after dinner. I asked Mike Masterson the other day what he dreamed about as a kid, expecting his stadium to be even grander than mine.

It wasn't, actually. Just the same fantasies of a kid standing alone aiming at the house, or in his case, the barn. The litany only in your head ... "the windup ... the pitch ... another strikeout, bringing to the end Masterson's third no-hitter." Only in your dreams.

I've talked to many players in a variety

of sports, and they all say the same thing. The dreams are what sustain them through the hard days, the losing streaks, the injuries.

There are hundreds of hockey players whose lonely, moonlit backyards resounded with the announcers detailing their goals. Football players who endured the eternal workouts, the endless strained muscles because of those dreams that took them home from the 50-yard line as the crowd went wild.

It's not just a male thing, these dreams. One of the best swimmers I've ever seen can relate in detail what the national anthem sounded like in those dreams she had. She knew the texture of the platform under her feet and the weight of the medal around her neck years before she made it to that first Olympics. In her dreams the hours spent in the pool pushed her toward one thing only. By the time she actually achieved it, the experience was an old friend.

Not all of our dreams translate to reality just as we dreamed them. For some of us that happens. For others, the dream is a little bit of hope we carry around like a worn clipping from the newspaper, to take out of our wallet and examine when things get rough.

Masterson's dreams, for example,

came to better fruition than mine. The only time I ever pitch a real game is when the television station's softball team is down to third string. Usually I'm out in the field, even on the team of weekend jocks I play with. Masterson has actually pitched one of those no-hitters in a real stadium.

Still, those dreams were powerful. They made a nine-year-old kid stand tall, squinting into the evening sun in a small town in Indiana. They gave me the inner life I needed to sustain myself through the rougher days of high school, the drive to self-motivate through college. I still recall them now.

Dreams help bring forth the reality we all strive for daily. For Mike Masterson, his dreams led directly to a concrete reality of pitching in the majors. For me, I still see that nine-year-old kid pause, gauge the right step to aim for, then throw.

Often, when I'm looking for the right word, weighing whether I should print something I've discovered about a player while digging for a story, that kid comes up in my memory. And just like him, I stand a little taller, adjust my cap, and try to give it my best throw. When I'm lucky, I hear that solid thwack, a thump just like the one of ball against step, telling me I've hit just the right place.

Only in my dreams. It has a nice ring to it. Because only in my dreams do I hit the step every time. However, in my reality I'm still striving for the same thing, and quite often I achieve it. Only in my dreams am I perfectly successful, but without those dreams reality would be a poor thing in comparison. I'll keep the dreams.

FOUR

Saturday morning. Meg sat curled up in her favorite chair, still in her pink nightshirt, hair tumbled in untidy curls around her shoulders, with all the things that constituted her Saturday morning ritual. None of them seemed the same. The coffee in her mug was cooling, and the powdered doughnuts of her once-a-week junk-food binge were getting stale. The television was off. Somehow she'd lost interest in the movie she had rented the night before. All that engaged her was the newspaper in her hand.

Alex had done it again. He hadn't lost that finesse. Now anyone *else* looking at that column would have said it was a nice piece of work. As far as she was concerned, Alex himself was the piece of work. She could see him leaning over his PC, smiling that one-cornered smile of his she knew so well while he crafted this one.

Meg read the story completely differently than the rest of the world did, and she knew that Alex had planned it that way. Other people reading this would see a vision of a skinny kid dreaming about being a baseball player and think what a swell guy Alex was. All Meg could see in her mind's eye was the look Alex had given her leaving the car yesterday. It was a wonder that the rain hadn't turned to steam when it hit him, he'd been so hot.

He'd said his dreams were powerful stuff that sustained him through the hard times. Meg knew hers this last week had been powerful, waking and sleeping. Since Alex had slipped back into her life, her dreams were charged with a voltage of unbelievable intensity.

The doorbell rang, startling Meg out of her thoughts. Looking through the peephole, all she could see was a gray, hooded sweatsuit. Craning her neck to look up further, she saw Alex.

"What are you doing here? How did you find my place to begin with?"

He walked through the door, looking around. "Good morning to you, too, Mutt. And, yes, I would like some of that coffee I smell brewing. Got any more doughnuts?"

"How did you know what I was having for breakfast? You can't smell doughnuts."

His thumb rubbed up against her cheek, dragging a shiver up her spine as the warm, slightly rough skin caressed hers. "No, but the powdered sugar is a dead giveaway."

"Oh." It was hard to come up with intelligent conversation with him this close. "Well, they're on the countertop in the kitchen. Plates are in the cabinet right above them.''

"Going somewhere?"

"What do you think?"

"That you won't get far dressed like that. It's no big thing anyway, Mutt. I've seen you in your nightie before.''

"Yeah, but that was back in a dorm when I slept in sweats.''

"Filled them out a bit differently, too. This . . . defies imagination.''

Alex's throaty chuckle followed her into the bedroom even after she slammed the door shut and started rummaging for clean blue jeans. Quickly rummaging. Alex was a gentleman, and he wouldn't dream of coming in here while she changed clothes. The only time he'd ever seen her underwear was when he'd bribed Cindi to let him into their room and then tacked the entire drawerful onto the ceiling of the hall outside.

No, not the only time. Her condition the next morning left no doubt that Alex had seen her in her underwear that night he put her to bed after the frat party. She couldn't face him again until she was behind several layers of fabric.

When she opened the door, he had made himself comfortable in her chair, watching Saturday morning cartoons, eating her doughnuts, and drinking her coffee. He looked over her jeans and shirt and seemed to approve.

"Do I need a ticket?"

"Excuse me?"

"For this charity thing you're roping me into. Do I need a ticket or a pass or something?"

"No, just tell your boss you're participating and we'll fix it up. It's black tie, though."

"No problem. I finally broke down and bought my own penguin suit last year. It was easier than going through all the rigamarole at the rental places every time we had a sports banquet."

"So did you come over here just for that, or were you out of coffee at home?" Meg sat on the arm of the chair and Alex automatically made room for her, moving his coffee and sliding an arm around her. She appreciated not sitting on a cup of coffee, but the arm she hadn't counted on. Of course, it would look funny if she jumped up right away, so she sat, willing herself not to react to the hand on her knee. It was only reflex anyway, she told herself.

"I had coffee. Needed it, too, after last night. I sat awake for a while, wondering if you were going to come get me when you read that column. Was it too obvious?"

"I should be thankful you didn't mention any names. A couple people at work have started calling me Mutt, Langdon," she said, rumpling the hair she knew he'd carefully blown dry. "I don't think it was too obvious. It was a good column, too."

"You think so? I didn't want to get too sentimental and all, but I've been doing so much hard-edged stuff lately that it was time for something softer."

"So you're telling me that even without my inspiration you probably would have tossed that one off yesterday? Thanks, pal." Meg gave his shoulder a playful shove. It was a mistake, she realized, because it just made him tighten that arm around her waist, nearly pulling her down into his lap.

"Now I didn't say that. I just said I was due for a softer column. Of course, you were terribly inspiring. You continue to . . . be an inspiration . . ." He pulled her the rest of the way into his lap.

The wall of his chest rose and fell. Meg didn't ever remember this chair being so comfortable before. Sitting in it on top of Alex should have been awkward and uncomfortable. Instead, it was a homecoming, getting sweeter with each minute. Listening to the tinny sound track of the cartoons in the background, smelling brewing coffee and Alex's cologne together seemed perfectly natural.

The naturalness of the feeling was what startled Meg, made her come fully awake to a realization as shocking as a glass of ice water in her face. This was her apartment, where she'd been happy and comfortable, alone, for nearly four years. In five minutes' time Alex had come in, made himself at home, and become part of the furnishings.

He wasn't going to do it again, Meg promised. There wasn't going to be another one of these one-sided romances with Alex. She slipped out of his embrace as he started trailing absent little kisses into her hair. "We cannot do this, Alex."

"We can't?" His constant answering with a question was infuriating. Almost as infuriating as the easy humor in his eyes when they met hers.

Meg could feel herself tense, arms folded across her chest as she looked at him. She couldn't say looked down at him, because sitting in the chair Alex was only slightly shorter than she was standing.

"It's a lot of fun, Alex, but we're playing with fire. And there's no good reason for it. I mean, we've always been friends."

"Right, if you don't count the last five years." Damn that smile, anyway.

"See, that's just what I meant. I'm not in love with you, Alex; you're not in love with me. I'm just happy we're speaking to each other. It beats exchanging Christmas cards."

Alex gave her a strange look. "I've never exchanged Christmas cards with you in my life, Mutt."

Meg felt her skin flush hot, then cold. "No?"

He shook his head. "Not me."

Her mind raced as she thought of a way to phrase her next question. "Um, Alex. When you were married, did you get all of your mail?"

He closed one eye, face rolling up in a wince. "Not exactly. Trudi always got home before I did and rifled through things. She hid what she thought I shouldn't see. I mean, the charge bills were out of sight. But that's not what we're talking about here, is it?"

"Not exactly. Let's just say I'm beginning to understand why you still feel like you have an apology coming."

Alex's face softened. "You wrote to me?"

Meg nodded, unsure that she could speak and put things into the right words. "And when all I got back was this stupid embossed Christmas card . . ."

Alex groaned. "That god-awful thing with the

blue and gold partridges. Not my idea. By then things were pretty shaky anyway, and Trudi would have cheerfully burned any correspondence from another woman."

His face cleared, and he was reaching for her hips to pull her back to him. "Sounds like we have some lost time to make up."

Meg moved back a step away from his persistent embrace. "I'm not ready to make up anything, Alex. Not yet. Right now I think we ought to work on just speaking to each other."

"Just speaking?"

She nodded. "Speak to each other, hopefully across rooms full of other people." Meg willed the pain out of her voice, banished the trembling. "I will not get involved with you again, Alex. It's too chancey, and too painful. I think for at least the next two weeks we ought to cool things off," Meg said, standing back to let him get out of the chair.

"Funny, I wasn't aware they were heating up yet," Alex said. Still, he picked up his dishes and put them down in the kitchen. Something unreadable was in his eyes as he went to the door. In anyone else except an egomaniac like Alex, Meg would have called it hurt. However, with Alex, she knew it was most likely theatrics.

"I'll talk to you on the phone, Alex. And I'll see you a week from Saturday at the benefit party, all right?"

"I guess so. Can we shake hands good-bye, Mutt?"

"Out of the question," she said, ushering him

through the door. Just the pressure of her hand in the small of his back, moving him gently out of her apartment was so tempting she could hardly stand it. Only when the lock clicked behind him did her pulse rate slow to normal.

"It isn't working."

Meg could sense Alex behind her, the nearness of him making the back of her neck tingle where the hair was swept up into a chignon. "What isn't working?"

"This staying apart stuff. There's got to be at least two hundred people in this room and I can only see you. How does that dress stay up, anyway? I mean, I can tell that stuff around your shoulders is just for show."

He was right. The short black sheath didn't get any support from the white chiffon and lace that circled low on her shoulders. When she'd chosen the dress, she'd wondered if it was too daring. With Alex and his appraisal in back of her, Meg was happy she'd worn it.

She turned to face him. "Trust you to ask a question like that, Alex. We both know it isn't my generous physical attributes. It's stuff called boning that runs up the sides and stiffens things."

"I'll say." His face was solemn except for the eyes, which were like sapphires, alight with his inward smile. "It's . . . perfect on you. I can't even call you Mutt when you're wearing that. Much too elegant. Settle for Maggie?"

"Not from anyone else. But from you it's acceptable."

"Thank you."

Meg looked at Alex. "That is undoubtedly the most unique formal wear in the room. Hawaiian print cummerband, Alex?"

"And tie to match. Had to have them specially made. But no one's denied me entrance to a party yet."

"Guess you just travel in the right circles. Having fun?"

"I am now. There isn't another soul here to talk to, you realize that? I mean, except for my boss, and I'd rather not. The less the two of us say to each other, the better. I gave him one of those little society waves across the room and he was satisfied."

Meg looked over the crowd. "You mean you haven't been attacked by autograph seekers? No debutantes pursuing your body?"

"None of them are fast enough. Besides, like I told you before, that little waiver thing I make them sign makes repeat dates unlikely."

"Right." Meg moved back a step to look at him judiciously. "You've got about ten minutes until you get up there and do your little stint at the podium. Ready?"

"Nerves, but nothing a good stiff drink wouldn't cure. How about you?"

"I'm fine. Of course, I'm not going up there." Meg looked across the room as the band stopped playing and a tall, slender woman tried to get the crowd's attention.

She and Alex moved toward the podium area to listen to all the introductions. Meg was glad that she'd asked Alex to be the first auctioneer of items donated for the benefit. That way she wouldn't have to baby-sit him all evening. Following Alex in a tuxedo was challenging to her sanity.

She wouldn't want to have to admit that it wasn't working for her either. Staying away from Alex for two weeks had only heightened her desire to call him. His picture still smiled from the newspaper, although developments in baseball had kept his column on real sports-related subjects for a change. And watching him on the news was even worse. Meg had never realized before just how well he came across on camera.

Finally it was Alex's turn to mount the platform to the podium. His hair glistened with golden highlights under the lights, and Meg wondered why the rush of pride and admiration came over her like a wave when the crowd laughed at his jokes. It wasn't as if there was any reason for her to be happy that they liked him. Not unless she actually cared about him, and what happened to him. And that just couldn't be possible.

Alex was trying to unfold a T-shirt autographed by a sports figure and bumping into the podium while he did it. He smiled and leaned over to the mike. "This is where I stop trying to be suave and ask my charming and talented assistant, Ms. M. Margaret Shepherd to come up here and display the . . . merchandise."

Meg froze amid the laughter. She knew everyone

was looking at her, and cold sweat misted her body. She started shaking her head slowly just as Mr. Harbison's gaze met hers. The motion he made pointing to the platform was unmistakable.

She didn't trip on the stairs, even though she could barely feel them under her heels. Methods for murdering Alex as soon as they both descended began to crowd out the panic in her chest. Alex motioned her up beside him and leaned over to speak in a voice no one but she could hear. "Don't worry, I'm not going to make you say a word. Just smile and hold this stuff, okay?" Alex winked at her, handing her the shirt.

Her reaction to that wink sent shivers twinkling down her spine and back up. But even more delighted shivers didn't banish Meg's aggravation. "You realize, of course, that once we get down from here, I'll have to kill you," she said, trying to keep a sweet smile while she muttered at him.

"You don't want to do that." His voice was smooth. "If you kill me, you won't know what Masterson had to say."

They auctioned off six items. At least, Meg thought it was six. She was so busy making sure her dress stayed put and running over in her mind the possibilities of Masterson's answer that she lost track of the auction. Alex's hand on her shoulder brought her out of her private thoughts. "We're done. You survived. Let's go."

There was a little applause as they went down the steps. Meg congratulated herself, again, on not tripping or doing anything else to make a fool of herself in public.

Alex led her swiftly far from the crowd. She followed with his arm curved in a gentlemanly fashion around her—at least it would have felt gentlemanly had it been anyone else's arm—up the stairs to the wide balcony of the ballroom.

"There's a bar up here," Alex explained. "You can wait one more minute. I need a beer."

They went to the bar, and Alex got a long-necked bottle and a glass. Meg glanced at the label. "You're still drinking that syrupy British stuff. Ugh."

"Keeps anybody from wanting a sip. Besides, I like it."

Leaning on the edge of the balcony, Meg watched him pour the liquid into the glass. She hadn't ever noticed before how much the deep amber fluid was the same color as Alex. The glinting highlights in his hair, the tan base of his neck that moved when he swallowed were all in harmony with the fluid.

So was the sharp, bitter taste that Meg knew was in the glass. That brew had as many sharp edges as the man drinking it, and now was not the time to get involved with either of them. She waited impatiently while half the glass disappeared. "Thank you. Auctioneering is thirsty work. Now, we were discussing . . ."

She couldn't resist a shove to his shoulder. "Masterson, Alex. What he said, as if you could forget."

"Well, you certainly can't. Your color's better now than when you were up on the platform, and that's saying something. I can see all those little freckles, Maggie, just like constellations."

She avoided the finger that reached out to connect the dots. "Cut it out, Alex. What did he say? Is he going to do it?"

The rest of the beer had disappeared, and Alex looked decidedly owlish already. "Maybe. I think he'd like to."

"But you don't know?"

"He's still thinking. Besides, he has conditions, some of which might be hard to meet."

He turned away from the edge of the balcony. "Wait a minute, where are you going?"

"To get another beer. This one's empty." Was he actually weaving that broadly? Meg felt herself growing uncomfortable. Alex's tolerance for beer had always been a school legend. Still, if she didn't know better, she'd say he was getting tipsy on one bottle.

There hadn't been any drinking before the auctioneering, of that she was certain. His breath close to her had been sweet and free of anything intoxicating, at least intoxicating to him. For her it had been a real debate as to whether to kiss him or smack him for finagling her up there.

He was back now, intent on pouring the liquid down the side of the glass. "Keeps the head manageable," he pontificated.

"So what are these unmanageable conditions, Alex? We've had celebrities in the hospital before, and I've never had a problem accommodating them."

His grin was lopsided. "I'll bet. You're so accommodating, Maggie." He put both his bottle and glass on a small table nearby and pulled her close to him, his back to the balcony. "Marvelously accommodating, aren't you? Want to do some accommodating right here on the balcony?"

She put her hands on his shoulders, keeping their bodies from meeting. "Alex, there are still people up here."

"You, me, a bartender. Not too many others. Just that guy with the lady who looks like she swallowed lemons."

"Alex, 'that guy' is my boss."

"And naturally the lady is his wife. Nobody would bother with somebody that homely otherwise. . . ."

"*Alex.*" It was hard to keep her voice down to a well-modulated low key. "You're drunk."

"Nonsense. I've had one and a half bottles of ale. Not enough to scratch the surface. I do feel pretty funny, though."

"I can tell. Could we possibly get back to discussing Bat Masterson and his conditions?"

"Doesn't have any conditions I know about. Healthy as a horse."

"No, his conditions for coming to the hospital to see Gabe," Meg prompted, easing Alex into a nearby chair. He sat heavily, staring at the white tablecloth as if he expected to see something written there.

"Oh, yeah. It will never work out. He wants complete secrecy."

"We can do that."

"No cameras."

"We can still do that."

"And me to go with him."

Meg paused. "Can we do that?"

Alex looked very solemn. "Sure. No problem. I just love using my spare time to baby-sit ball players."

"All right, Langdon, what's going on here?" Meg grasped his arm. "Are you ill or something?"

"Has to be or something," Alex said, weaving slightly in his chair. "Maybe it was something in the fluoride."

"Excuse me?"

"You know, that nasty stuff the dentist puts on your teeth."

"I know what you mean, but I'm a little confused," Meg said.

"Went to the dentist this afternoon. Everything was juuuust wonderful." He smiled beautifully, steepling his fingers on the table. It would have been a more effective gesture if he hadn't missed the first time. "Don't have to go back for a year."

Memories were beginning to dawn on Meg. "You still have a lot of trouble going to the dentist, I'll bet."

"The worst. But I just call a couple days beforehand and get my prescription filled, and then I march in and get tortured like a good boy."

"Prescription? Like something to relax you in the chair?" Meg prompted, trying to get Alex's attention back from his slow lean over the balcony rail to watch a woman in a deeply cut cocktail dress walk by below.

"Yep. Like something to relax me."

"And you took one this morning?"

"Two. One this morning, then they called and said Dr. Doom was running late and could I come in later, so I took another one after lunch and marched right over to the firing squad." He smiled. "They missed."

Meg grimaced. "I'd say they were right on target. Alex, don't you know what that stuff probably is? Valium, or some other tranquilizer. You can't drink while you're on them."

"But I'm not on them. I haven't taken any since this afternoon." He leaned back. "Least I don't think so." There was a tiny hiccup.

"You don't even take aspirin for a headache, Langdon. With your lousy tolerance for medication, you shouldn't even have had a drink tomorrow, probably. Now what am I going to do with you?"

"I've got an idea."

"I'll bet you just do. Why don't you just stay real comfortable right there, and I'll be right back."

Meg watched Alex over her shoulder about every twenty steps. He sat, twirling the paper umbrella in the soda she'd gotten him before she left, cautioning the bartender not to give him anything else. Mercifully, Kim answered on the first ring.

She kept quiet while Meg explained. "Now what do I do with him?"

"Fluids. Plenty of noncaffeinated fluids to push that stuff on through. And once you get him home . . . you are taking him home, aren't you?"

Meg sighed. This was all beginning to feel very

familiar, but somehow skewed. Had Alex felt this way, getting her home from that awful frat party? "I guess I am."

"Well, let him sleep. He's going to feel rotten tomorrow, but he'll survive, Meg. Call me later, okay?"

Meg replaced the receiver in its cradle and went to say her good-byes and find Alex.

"Come on, Langdon, I'm taking you home."

His smile was broad. "Great. I knew I was more fun than the party."

Getting Alex into the car was a challenge. Meg guided him gently, making sure he didn't bang his head on the doorframe. Even more challenging was getting his seat belt buckled.

She hadn't realized what a vulnerable position she'd be in, leaning over the passenger side of the small car until Alex reached out and engulfed her. In an instant she was in his lap.

"None of this, my friend. I've got to get you home."

"But the night is still young." His voice was slow. "Surely we can dally a minute here."

"Not with my feet hanging out an open car door, Alex." Besides, crushed into his arms in the tight confines, Meg was beginning to discover just how little there was to her dress, how the fabric let the warmth of him engulf her. She extricated herself from his arms and closed the door behind her.

Adjusting the shoulders of her dress, she walked around the car, thankful for the cool night air. Slipping into the driver's seat, she started the car and got going quickly.

They went through the drive-through at a fast-food place a few blocks over. Meg got two large soft drinks and handed one to Alex. "Drink this. Now, with no arguments." Surprisingly, he acquiesced.

Alex's apartment building a few blocks from the TV station, and only a few miles from the hotel, was one of those nondescript structures that always made Meg think of egg crates. She got him out of the car without too much trouble. Alex was alternately humming and singing the old song that had been on the car radio.

"There," he said, opening the door to the apartment with a flourish.

"I'm so proud of you. And after only four tries." Of course, that didn't include the fishing for the keys in the elevator. Meg was glad there had been no one else to see her helping him go through his pants pockets.

The apartment was what she would have expected, had she thought. One very modern lamp cast a small puddle of light in the corner of the white box that was the living room. A black metal arrangement of modern shelves housed a very large television and other expensive audio and video equipment. Other than an aquarium on its own metal stand, the only furnishings in the room were a stark painting of a city skyline in black, red, and white and an exercise bike.

"So this is your place," Meg said. Alex laughed,

a sound that rumbled out of his chest as he leaned against the door frame.

"Know what? I've been wondering what you'd say. Even you, Maggie, couldn't say 'nice place' about this. All the way over from the party, I've been thinking. What will tactful, generous Mutt say about my apartment? At least all the junk-food wrappers and newspapers got picked up yesterday."

Meg snorted. "No thanks to you, I'll wager."

He raised an index finger and waggled it at her. "Give the lady a teddy bear, folks, she's hit the bull's-eye. You're absolutely right. I have a cleaning service."

Meg looked around the room again and focused on the aquarium. The dull silver bodies passing each other, small eyes and low, underslung jaws fascinated her. She looked again. "Langdon, those are piranhas."

"Aluminum fish. It's illegal to own piranhas. So they're aluminum fish, least if anybody asks. Of course, if nobody asks, they're still piranhas. Trudi and Maxwell."

Meg stifled a laugh that she couldn't keep totally quiet. "I get half the joke. Who's Maxwell?"

"He's the big guy. Trudi's divorce lawyer." With that he turned and moved down the short hallway that Meg could only assume led to the bedroom. He trailed fingers down the wall like a homing device, trying to stay upright and on track.

Meg could feel a massive urge to bolt and run. It was like déjà vu turned inside out, remembering that incident in her dorm room but being on the other side. Maybe this was her payback for all that fraternity beer. "Well, it's been quite an evening, she began. "I've gotten you home now, so I'll just see myself out. Make sure the door's locked behind me, okay. Alex?"

He paused at the doorway to the bedroom, looking mournful. "I can't untie my tie. And I can't get these damned little studs out. Fingers won't work. Do you really want me to have to sleep in all of this, Maggie?"

The thought of undressing Alex tonight was almost more than she could take. Of course, the thought of him sleeping in a tux, rolling over on all those little metal studs, nagged at her conscience. She would grit her teeth and get on with it, Meg decided.

"Get in there and sit down," she said. The bedroom, at least, had furniture in it. There was a waterbed in a teak frame and a chest to match. On the top was an assortment of change, trinkets, ticket stubs, and tie tacks. There was no chair. Alex sat on the edge of the softly waving bed, looking as though he regretted the motion. His tux jacket was more or less folded on the floor beside him. Meg picked it up, going to the walk-in closet for a hanger.

Being in there was like being surrounded by a small room full of Alex. The smell of his cologne welled up, and Meg fought the urge to bury her face in a sweater and savor the scent that was uniquely his. But that would muss the fold, and everything in the closet was arranged so perfectly she knew that would never do. She hung the jacket and switched off the light in the closet.

At the bed, she turned back to work on Alex. As soon as she got her hands to his neck to work on the tie, his arms were around her. They stayed, running slow patterns up and down her back as she took the studs from the front of his shirt, slowly revealing a growing mat of dark golden chest hair.

Meg knew she had to have seen Alex without a shirt on before. But she'd never seen him in quite this fashion. Only in sophomoric college dreams had she ever undressed Alex. The reality was ten times better, or worse. His chest was broad, the muscles well defined under the golden hair her fingers yearned to stroke. The hair narrowed to a line just at the point where she couldn't undo any more buttons without unfastening his cummerbund and getting herself in serious trouble. And as much as that trouble beckoned, she was not going to go any farther with Alex, especially the fuzzy, drunken Alex sitting expectantly at the edge of the bed.

"Okay, pull it out yourself," she said before realizing what he might infer from her remark. The blush was impossible to stop and felt as if it came from the level of the white froth of chiffon around her shoulders. "The shirttail, Langdon, and the cummerbund. Now."

"Anything, Maggie. I'll be a very good boy, just for you." His voice was slow and husky, and he seemed to be humming under his breath the refrain of an old song, the one they'd heard on the radio. When he unfastened the cummerbund, his arms reaching behind his back flexed all his chest muscles until Meg was nearly against his chest, swallowing as her throat constricted with the nearness of him.

Then the fabric fell away and Alex relaxed, pulling his shirttail out of the black pants. She knelt and undid the last two studs, setting them all in a pile next to the bed. She was sweating from the effort of keeping her hands where they belonged. Never again would she hate Alex for vaulting through that window. Heck, she'd do it herself right now if she could, and they were probably twelve stories up.

Maybe she could be more conventional and just find the door. "You're on your own now, pal. This is where I quit." She put her hands on the side rail of the bed to stand up, quite a task in the narrow sheath.

"Oh, sweet Maggie. Don't leave just yet." Alex's hands roved her back again, then he pulled her close.

There was no barrier between them now except the bodice of her dress. She could feel the hair on his chest, crisp and plentiful as she put up a hand to forestall his embrace. She could have more easily stopped gravity.

Like a natural force, Alex gently engulfed her, sought her mouth, kissed her sweetly and deeply into a drunkenness to match his own. After a few moments Meg became aware that her chignon was now half undone, with curls snaking down her back.

Under her fingers Meg could feel Alex's heart beating, and a nipple as stiff and taut as her own had become apparent beneath the fabric of her sheath. She shivered in anticipation as he kissed her again, then moved his hot mouth down to the the junction of fabric and skin at her breastbone. Meg arched as his tongue found sensitive flesh, arcing her body back into the pressure of his firm hands behind her. One of those hands swiftly found the zipper in the back of the dress and slid it halfway down before Meg got her wits about her. His fingers traced down her spine and she fought to remember words, any words, that would keep her from leaning forward into him.

"No, Alex. We can't. You're drunk. Very, very drunk."

"And very, very besotted, Maggie. Can't you tell, woman? Nobody else ever felt like this, tasted like this."

Maggie wanted Alex to continue more than she had ever wanted anything, but she knew it was time to call a halt. If she didn't, she would always wonder if Alex sober would have been as warm and willing as Alex sozzled. That thought washed over her and traveled with shock waves down to her toes and back.

For a brief moment she was in a dormitory room with cinder block walls and a funny overhead light. The glow of it illuminated a very young woman cursing her would-be lover for his desertion.

The final realization that there had been no desertion, ever, made Meg's head spin. But trying to extricate herself just put her deeper into Alex's arms. She wondered if it had been as painful for him to tuck her in and boost himself out the window as it was going to be for her to ease his warm hands off her and head for the door.

He didn't release her until she firmly but gently pulled away, putting a knee on the bed frame for leverage.

"This is not to be, not tonight, Alex," she said softly, trying to recapture some dignity as she zipped up her dress and tucked her hair behind her shoulder. "Maybe it's just the heat of the moment."

"It's not the heat, it's the humidity," Alex said sagely. Meg didn't have time to contemplate that or her other thoughts before he put a hand on either side of him and tried to push off and stand.

"Where are you going?"

"Gotta feed the fish before bedtime. Don't want poor little Trudi and Maxwell to starve to death."

"I'll feed them. You get your pajamas on."

Meg walked into the living room, grateful for the distance between them. She looked around the aquarium stand. Frowning, she made a quick inventory of the kitchen cabinets before she went back to the bedroom to admit defeat.

"Alex, there's no fish food. Not for the . . . aluminum fish or those little goldfish in the bowl on the second shelf, either."

"There's no goldfish food because the goldfish *are* the food, Maggie," Alex said patiently.

"Oh, no. You feed those poor little things to the piranhas? Alex, I can't do that."

"But if you don't feed them, Maxwell will want a midnight snack. And then he'll eat Trudi." He paused in inebriated revery. "Or at least part of her. I don't think even Maxwell is that much of a pig."

Meg suppressed a sigh. "Okay, I'll feed them. Just get busy with those pajamas, okay?"

She went back into the living room and found the net beside the goldfish bowl. Scooping out two of the fish, she looked only long enough to lift the lid on the tank, plop them in, and listen for the closure of the lid before dropping the net and leaving the room without a backward glance. *The things we do for love*, she thought, walking down the hall.

Love. The word, even unspoken in her mind, stopped Meg in the middle of Alex's short hallway. There, it was out and she could admit it. She loved Alex Langdon. She had loved him five years ago and nothing in between mattered anymore. It was impossible for Meg to deny she loved him now.

And tonight she loved him enough to tuck him in and walk away. He still sat on the edge of the bed, sans trousers, sans socks. His briefs were tiny, navy blue and white striped, and obviously constricting after the last few minutes. "Don't own any pajamas. But I didn't think you really wanted to see my normal sleeping attire, or lack of it."

Meg stopped where she was at the doorway. "You're right. Good night, Alex. I'll let myself out."

His brow puckered. "No good-night kiss?"

"Definitely not."

"How 'bout a drink of water and a bedtime story?"

Why didn't he just rip the skin off her and get it over with? Meg shook her head. "Langdon, I'm out of here."

"How 'bout just the drink. I really am still thirsty, Maggie."

Sighing, she went into the bathroom, drew a glass of water, and went back. He lay on the bed now, looking drowsy and obedient. He propped his head up on one elbow and drank thirstily, draining the glass. "Tuck me in? I can't find the sheet."

The man was determined to destroy her sanity. "You're on top of it. Roll over and I'll help."

Alex obeyed, on the edge of sleep. He curled one arm around her knees as Meg tucked him in, and he gave a low growl. "Just figured it out."

"Figured what out, Alex?"

"Why Trudi never felt right. She wasn't you."

Meg couldn't answer that. Just hearing it made her breathing get all funny again. It would be easier to take the statement seriously if Alex's hand hadn't slipped off her knees as he drifted off.

"Maggie . . ."

"Yes, Alex."

"There's a spare key in the kitchen junk drawer. It's the only key 'cept for the car ones. And Maggie?"

From Alex the repetition of a name that usually made her cringe was like a caress. "Yes?"

"Thank you. I . . . really appreciate this." He squeezed her hand, then dropped his fingers limply to the sheet. "Love you," he muttered before he dozed off.

"You are going to be so sorry tomorrow, Alex, my love," she said softly as she turned out the light and went down the hall. The key was just where he said it would be. Even through the haze of tears Meg found it.

So Alex had said he loved her. Damn shame it was a drunken reflex to being tucked in, and she was never going to hear it from him sober. It was the ultimate irony contrasting tonight with that debacle in her dorm room.

Meg walked through the darkened apartment and locked the door behind her. She rode down the elevator in silence except for her own humming. It was a slow, minor-keyed thoughtful version of a very old song that would always now bring to her the scent and sound and taste of Alex. After tonight she knew the taste would still be honey but with an edge of bitterness.

THE MORNING STAR   SECTION D
COMMENTARY
Alex Langdon

I'm really feeling stupid this morning. Gullible, too. Many people would agree with both of those statements, but I tend to think of myself as neither, most of the time.

However, this morning both apply. This is the same man who did an entire series of columns and who reports on the evening news on the inane reasons most players give for getting hooked on drugs or alcohol. And when one of the leading players on our city's baseball team got a DWI arrest during spring training, I was the one who leaned on him the hardest.

There is no excuse for such stupidity, I said. Any sane adult can stay away from alcohol and drugs. Any responsible grown-up can stay straight and still have a good time.

Perhaps any responsible grown-up can. If asked Saturday before noon, I would have certainly said I could have. This morning's throbbing head and aching body remind me that I would have to retract that statement if I want to stay honest.

Okay, so there is still no excuse for drinking, or using mind-altering substances of any kind, and driving. Or flying. Or playing baseball, for that matter. However, it is possible to screw up just as completely as some national sports figures have with alcohol or drugs and not realize what you're getting yourself into. I know, because Saturday I think I did it.

I say I think I did that because Saturday is kind of fuzzy. I know that I ingested a couple of tranquilizers Saturday during the daylight hours. That was to get through a nasty visit to the dentist. (In my book, there isn't such a thing as a non-nasty visit to the dentist's office. Sorry, Doc.)

I didn't think anything about it. Sit in

dentist's chair, pop pills first. That's the
way life goes for me. Then Saturday
night, having totally forgotten that those
little pills were still swimming around
in my blood stream, I went to a party
and had a couple of beers.

Then I made a complete and total fool
of myself. Thankfully, I have friends who
can recognize that fact better than I can,
and someone drove me home. Someone
undressed me. Someone fed my fish. All
I did was the real intelligent stuff like
make cow eyes at a woman and sing a
few old songs. If my neighbors heard all
that, I'm sorry.

The point of all that is, I didn't realize
what I was doing until it was already
done. That doesn't make me intelligent,
only human. And I now can figure out
how it is that those fellows quoted the
day after some really stupid incident on
the field or in an automobile can say, "I
don't know what happened. I don't usually do that." They probably really don't.

"I didn't know what I was doing."
What an insane statement, I would have
said before Saturday. Of course they
knew what they were doing. A person is
in control of what his body does, so he's
the responsible party when that body
drives a car into someone, or destroys a
locker room, or any of the other stupid

offenses I've railed over coming from anyone else. But maybe that's the big problem. Some of these guys honestly don't know what they are doing. And no one has ever stopped them, when they're back in a rational mind-set, to point out what they're doing.

No one had to point out much to me. It was easy to figure out very quickly. My apartment was a wreck, and I was worse. A call to my doctor told me I wasn't going to die, although he did have some choice words for me. By mid-afternoon Sunday I almost felt human again.

I do know something. Once is enough, at least for me. I will not be refilling that prescription for tranquilizers unless I plan to forget booze for a couple of days before and after the next time I sit in Dr. Doom's dental gallery of horrors. And perhaps I will be a little more forgiving to the guys who have an occasional lapse.

I will be even more forgiving of the people who actually do something about their problems. This morning that tranquilizer bottle is empty, the contents having been flushed somewhere between my third and fourth quart of ice water Sunday. As stupid as I will feel, I'll be adding a recap of the incident to my lecture the next time I'm speaking at a high school. Perhaps it will make a few people sit up and take notice before they have to deal with this problem on a firsthand basis.

Of course, some friends would remind me that the easiest answer is not to bother with substances that are abusable in the first place. Mike Masterson happened to call while I was in the throes of my agony, and by the time I was done talking to him, expecting just a little sympathy, he was laughing so hard he had trouble holding on to the telephone. He reminded me it's hard to get as miserable as I was when one's drink of choice is diet cola. Score one for the Batman.

Some things change quite a bit in 24 or 48 hours. I will no longer write scathing commentaries on players who have substance problems without asking myself once what led to those problems and what they might be doing about them. And for anyone with whom I spoke after eight P.M. Saturday, I'll rephrase a little of what my television station puts on the air after the crackpots are allowed an editorial. Statements expressed by the gentleman inhabiting my body do not necessarily reflect the opinions of the management. Thank you.

Meg was deep into writing a press release on the hospital's new safety seat program when the phone on her desk rang. "Margaret Shepherd."

"Alex Langdon."

Meg went on writing her press release, aggravated that her heart still gave that little flop in her chest at his voice. "Oh, are we still speaking?"

"I dunno. Was I that obnoxious Saturday night?"

Meg flashed with irritation. Obnoxious is the last thing she would have called Alex Saturday night. Tender, sweet, perhaps even loving. But he'd made it perfectly clear in his column that none of that was real. "Not as obnoxious as you were this morning in print, Langdon."

"Oh, come on. I was all right. I was okay Saturday, too, I'll bet. You probably drove me home just for show."

"Right, Alex. You couldn't even tie your own shoes Saturday night."

"I couldn't do it Sunday morning either. My head wouldn't let me bend over that far. I have never felt like that in my entire life."

"Not even after that kegger after the bed race?"

"I was not the one who was drunk that night, Maggie. Not by a long shot."

Meg took the lid off the jar of chocolate-covered raisins, which were calling to her from the sheer stress of having this conversation. "I know. But you sure were Saturday night."

"Yeah, but I'm cute. And I talked to Masterson, too. Want to hear what he said?"

She dropped her handful of candy back into the jar. "Of course I do, you fool. Tell me."

"Huh uh. Not now. Tonight at Tony's Pizza, corner of Twelfth and Jefferson. We can all three have a cozy little chat. Seven P.M."

"Fine. I'll see you then."

"Great. And Maggie?"

"Yes, Alex."

"I'm sorry if I was obnoxious, this morning or Saturday." The phone went dead before Meg could reply.

So Alex thought he'd been obnoxious Saturday night. She wondered how much he remembered. She remembered plenty, including her realization that she was still in love with him. Even that dreadful tag line in his column about "opinions of the management" couldn't change that, much as she wished it did. Somewhere, under all the arrogance, was the man who looked like Alex had Saturday night when he drifted off, still holding her hand. Meg wondered if she'd ever meet that man again. The press release was half completed, the screen of her PC mocking her with its empty black space and blinking green square. She dipped into the chocolate-covered raisins.

"No cameras."

"Fine."

"And no advance publicity of any kind."

"I'll tell the boy and his parents that nobody else is to know. Believe me, we can trust them. I'll give you their home phone number if you want it. They'll cooperate." Meg settled herself into the booth at the restaurant, trying to get comfortable next to Alex. If she got as comfortable as she would have liked, they'd never finish the business at hand.

Across from her, the ball player nodded. "I might like to do that. Alex says they're from near my old stomping grounds in Union. I think you're right. We can trust them."

"Anything else? I can arrange for security to let you in a freight entrance if you want, ride up the personnel elevator."

Masterson grimaced. "I'm not the president or anything. I just don't want any media types around, other than Alex here."

"And he's agreed to come?" Meg still remembered Alex's snide remark about baby-sitting ball players.

Alex draped a heavy arm around her shoulder. "Don't talk about me like I'm not here, Maggie. I'm coming. I won't stay forever, but I'm coming."

Meg took a sip of her diet cola. "Okay. Great. So I'll get it set up." She leaned on Alex's shoulder. It felt cozy to settle in next to him. It would have felt cozier if Alex hadn't been a little tense about something. The muscles in his arm were stiff against her body. However, she knew his enjoyment of her touch probably didn't extend to her massaging his shoulders in public, so she let it ride. Even so, Masterson's eyebrows shot up.

"Favor to an old friend, huh, Langdon?"

Alex grinned. "The oldest and the best. Would I go to such elaborate means to set up anyone else?"

Masterson shook his head, looking at Meg. "I guess not. I'm sorry about that, by the way. I really didn't know about the guys on the other side of the door with the cameras."

Meg managed a wave. "That's all right. It's over now, and it won't be repeated, and I kind of had it coming."

A grin quirked Mike's face. "You really set fire to his news copy?"

Meg nodded. "And he wasn't as cool as it sounded in that column either. He about had a stroke."

Alex grimaced. "And what I did to deserve it, I'll never know."

Meg could only look at him in amazement. Jumping out the window of her dorm room she wouldn't mention in public, but there was plenty that she could. "Alex, you'd tacked all my underwear to the ceiling of the residence hall just the week before, just to mention one incident. Isn't that deserving of something?"

"Hanging," Masterson said as the waitress set down a steaming pizza. "Can you people stop squabbling long enough to eat, or is this mine?"

"We'll eat," Alex said, grabbing a plate. "Never leave this man alone with food, Maggie. Not if you want anything to eat."

"You're exaggerating," Masterson said. "Just because of that one steak. . . ."

The pizza was gone, and they were all leaning back, rolling ice around in their glasses, before anyone spoke again. Alex looked at his watch. "I've got about ten minutes left before I have to be back to the station. See you guys later."

Meg started up after him. "Wait a second, I almost forgot. I've still got your key."

"Keep it," Alex said, putting down a tip on the table. "Never know when it might come in handy."

Meg flushed at the roguish look on his face. "I'd feel better if I didn't," Meg said, slipping the key into his shirt pocket.

"Have it your way." He dropped a brief kiss on her cheek. "See you."

"See you," she echoed, watching him leave. It surprised her when she realized she had one hand on her cheek, protecting the spot where he'd kissed her. If Masterson's eyebrows had been raised before, they were almost in his hairline now.

"Wow, this is getting interesting."

Meg sat down again, trying to stay calm. "What

makes you say that? Surely there are enough women clustered around Alex. . . ."

"Clustered, at a distance," the ball player said. "They buzz around, but nobody lights. Getting the key to Casa Langdon is serious."

"Sure. Just as serious as he was when he set me up to walk in on you."

"Probably. He was pretty serious about that. Took some major planning, you'll have to admit." Meg decided she liked Masterson's smile. It reminded her of Gabe when he was well enough to cook up trouble. "See, Alex and I have a pact going. I keep saying 'no comment' and he keeps saying 'no commitment.' "

Meg laughed. It was better than crying. "Don't worry. There's no commitment yet." *And not likely to be any,* she added to herself.

Masterson pulled out his wallet. Meg wrinkled her brow. "What are you doing with that?"

He seemed to blush a little under the spring-training tan. "I don't let ladies take me to dinner, normally."

"You ought to when they're asking as big a favor of you as I am. Put it away this time. Some other time I'll let you treat. Maybe in the hospital cafeteria after you visit Gabe."

Masterson stuck out a hand for a handshake. "Done."

Ever the country gentleman, he saw her to her car. Meg was still wondering at that handshake. It was warm and friendly and did absolutely nothing for her. Every waitress in the restaurant would have traded a week's tips for that handshake, and she had gotten it for free and not cared. No doubt about it, she was in over her head with Alex.

The next morning Meg dressed with Gabe in mind. She was looking forward to telling him about Masterson. She tied her hair back with a fat bow and put on a white blouse with a lace collar and his favorite blue jumper. Today would be Gabriel's day.

It was almost ten in the morning before she got to his room. When she did, Spence was there, looking serious, along with Liz, who looked positively grim. Gabe was sleeping, fitfully. Spence drew her out in the hallway, Liz following him.

"All of a sudden, that last skin graft isn't doing so well. It's trying to infect itself right off his body, I think," Spence said.

A look at Liz confirmed it. "We may have to do bone scans to make sure the infection isn't going deeper."

Meg winced. "I was hoping you guys wouldn't have to go through this again. When he wakes up, call me back. I've got something to tell him."

Liz looked protective. "Good news, I hope?"

"The best, but I want to tell him first."

"Fine with me," Spence said. "Maybe we can get him to eat lunch."

Lunch, when it arrived in Gabe's room just as Meg did, was not entertaining. "Oh, boy, rubber Jell-O," Gabe said, his voice as flat as the dish of gelatin.

Meg was surprised to see how his cheekbones threatened to poke through the skin more so than four days earlier. When he reached for a carton of milk, she could see bone so prominently at his wrist it made her ache.

She forced cheerfulness into her voice. "Hey, sport, I don't have to ask if you're sitting down for this, but hold onto that rail, okay? You're going to have a visitor Friday."

"Oh, great. You get that tutor lined up to torture me through geometry?" He poked at the gelatin, watching it move around in green waves.

"Not exactly. This is more in the line of a social call. Three guesses."

His eyes crinkled and Gabe came as close to a sneer as she'd ever seen. "Friday. Must be the guys from the baseball team again, rubbing it in that they're still winning without me."

"Not exactly."

"I don't think I'm up to the cheerleaders."

"They aren't coming either. Think hard."

"Crud, I don't know. The Easter Bunny. Bat Masterson. Superman."

"Well, one out of three isn't bad."

Gabe fell back on the pillow. "Come on, Meg, I'm too old for that. Let the little kids go down to the dayroom and hunt eggs."

"Easter was last week, Gabriel. Masterson's going to be here at ten A.M."

His eyes widened, and the straw he'd been using to torture the gelatin fell to the tray. "No joke?"

She looked at his brown eyes, widening in the pale face. "No joke."

Meg hadn't expected the tears. Just two of them

pooled out and slid down his cheeks before he turned away. "Oh, Gabe," she said softly. "Don't."

"I just can't believe it. Bat Masterson, coming here." He swiped a bony hand across his face and looked down at his tray. "Guess I'm going to have to eat this slime, huh? I want to be able to stand up to meet him." He took a deep breath and smiled.

Meg and Spence exchanged glances. Spence actually winked at her. He followed her out of the room as she left. At the doorway she looked over her shoulder at Gabe. He was already digging into his lunch, sports page in one hand, spoon in the other.

Spence handed her his handkerchief. It was shining white and felt as if it had been dried outside on a clothesline. She leaned against the wall and covered her face with it, trying to cry quietly. "I'm sure that was hard to set up, Meg. Thank you. Gabe will thank you too, once he comes down to earth."

"I've got all the thanks I need," she said, wiping her eyes and handing back the handkerchief.

Spence folded it and put it in the pocket of his jeans. "I've been reading that sports page too, Ms. Shepherd. Are congratulations of some type in order? It seems you have yourself a serious beau."

"Beau, perhaps. Alex Langdon has never been serious. You'll get to meet him, anyway. He's coming in with Masterson on Friday for moral support."

"Good. I'll make sure his intentions are honorable," Spence said, laughing when he made a face at him.

"You do that, Spence, you just do that. I want to hear what he says."

*   *   *

Meg's lunch was stuff out of the vending machine, grabbed while she worked. The work just seemed to pile up sometimes. There were school tours to set up, résumés to collect from a few new staff members so that she could write press releases making them sound like candidates for the Nobel Prize for medicine, and plenty of other little goodies that demanded her immediate attention.

The level lowered dangerously in the raisin jar. She was going to have to go grocery shopping, probably before Saturday. Drat. Then the call she always hated came, about three P.M.

It was the emergency room. "The police are here. Once the radios get busy, all the reporters will show up. We need you down here, Meg. This one is bad."

The toddler who had been brought in by ambulance was tiny and too brutalized to even scream as the staff stuck needles in her, checked her vital signs, and whisked her into a room. The young police officer who'd been in the ambulance was pounding a wall as he watched the doctors and nurses swarm around the tiny body. "Do you know what he told me?" He addressed Meg because she was the closest. "That she must have fallen off the bed. Dammit, can't they figure out that no baby falls off a bed and looks like that?"

By the time the mother came in, pale and tall, but fine-boned like her daughter, Meg had rebuffed the earliest reporters, gotten the police officer a cup of coffee, and found him a seat where he could wait. He set down the coffee and went to talk to the woman, who flew past him after a few words and tried to break the circle of people around the tiny body.

She was sent away, gently. One of the interns came out to talk to her a moment, then she slumped into a chair, tears almost unnoticed as they trailed down her face. The officer was as gentle as he could be as he questioned her. Did she usually leave the child with her boyfriend while she worked? Had anything happened before?

The woman sat silent a long time. Meg controlled her nausea. It always came, unbidden, when she had to do this. Of all the parts of her job, this was the worst. This part almost made her wish she had tried reporting. Or digging ditches. Or anything. Finally the woman spoke, in broken sentences. "I got no other baby-sitter. Not with Jimmy out of work. She . . . gets into everything. Runs away from him, on purpose. You know? He says she needs to mind." She fell silent, twisting one corner of the shirt she wore over a faded tank top.

Meg left the room. The excuses, the justifications drove her to the brink of insanity. Back on her floor she went to her desk, grabbed her coffee cup, and filled it with ice and water, gulping the liquid down. There were several messages. She sifted through them. Most could wait. Alex had called twice. She bit her lip. She ought to call him, but she didn't want him to hear her the way she would sound right now. As she debated, the phone rang and reflexively she answered it.

"Hi, you, it's me. Want to do dinner on my break?"

"Not tonight. I'm going to be here a long time."

"Maggie, what's wrong? You sound awful."

"We've got some heavy stuff going on here. I have to go back down to the emergency room. Talk to you later, okay?"

Before he could argue, she hung up, heading for the elevator. When she got downstairs, the officer was still there, quietly questioning the woman. Five feet from them a crew worked to save her toddler. One limp, chubby hand draped off the table. There were scratches on the back of the hand among the dimples, and Meg shivered. It was going to be a long evening.

The child and the crew around her went upstairs together, to surgery. Most of the doctors and nurses came down in twos and threes, avoiding the corner where the officer and the child's mother sat. Meg sat with them. About six o'clock, an older man, gray at the temples, came down alone. One look at his face told Meg everything she needed to know.

Not fifteen minutes later people with video cameras were trickling into the emergency room. Others, with notebooks, gathered with them. Meg was alone with them, the officer and his charge having fled into a secluded area while the necessary forms and reports were completed. Later, Meg would find them a way out of the hospital.

"Now you guys know we may not have an official statement for hours yet. Why come every time and camp out here?" Meg asked tiredly.

"It's our job. You do yours, we do ours. What can you say right now?"

"You know she can't say a damned thing," a deep voice growled at Meg's side.

"Hey, Langdon, you're supposed to be on our side," someone called from the back of the press of bodies. "What gives?"

"What gives is the lady needs about fifteen minutes to compose herself and figure out what to give you vultures. I figured she might need an armed guard to be allowed to do that. Now I'm not armed, but I am dangerous." His glittering smile proved it as he whisked Meg into the elevator.

When the doors closed behind them, he gathered her into a bear hug. Tucked into his body, with her head on his chest, his chin shielding the top of her head, Meg didn't say a word. She just clung there, holding on tightly.

He broke the embrace when the elevator stopped on her floor. "Come on, let's get out now. I can only keep that bunch at bay for a little while. You're going to have to come up with something to give them." Meg started to say something and then stopped. Alex looked odd. There was a tautness to his cheek muscles and a pallor to his skin that she didn't like.

Maybe it was just the lighting in here, she told herself. Meg steadied herself against the wall of the elevator and stepped out. The floor of offices was empty and quiet for the most part. Normally the business staff at the hospital kept regular hours, and those hours had been over for a while.

"Why did you come?" she asked, sliding into her chair. Alex grabbed one from the next desk and sat down beside her.

"After I talked to you the last time, I saw Janice heading out. When they send her someplace, it means a hot story. She makes Trudi and Maxwell look like guppies. The assignment board said she was coming here, so I thought you might want company."

"Do I ever. This is the rough part."

His face was pale and very solemn. "I can't even imagine it. How can you do this? Surely it's harder than being on camera as a reporter."

"Yeah, but it's just part of the job. The other parts are great. Like setting up this thing for Gabe. He is so excited."

"Doesn't that bother you even more? Watching people sweat blood all day to make children live, then having somebody snuff one out like a bug?"

Meg shuddered. "Don't talk about it that way, okay? I don't handle things like that well, and I've still got work to do."

"Sorry." Alex sat silently and watched her while she made telephone calls, worked on a statement, called the police officer's supervisor to clear things with him, then finally called Mr. Harbison at home to read the finished copy to him before she went downstairs.

When everyone could agree, from the police to her boss, Meg printed out a copy of the brief statement. It was so stark. A Caucasian female child, aged twenty months, and so on and so on. Police say charges will be filed against the adult male who was caring for the child while her mother worked. End of statement. All that was left of a little elf with blond hair and dimples on her chubby hands.

Reading it back was too much. The nausea and the pain fought, and the nausea won. Meg dashed for the ladies' room. When she came out, a cold, moist paper towel still clutched in one hand, Alex was there, a can of lemon soda in hand.

"Sips. Small ones, and no argument," he said. "We ought to buy stock in the company. We seem to be using their product a lot."

"Yeah, but I'll feel a whole lot better tomorrow than you did Sunday," Meg said weakly. She took the can and did as Alex ordered. It was odd to see him acting like a mother hen. There was none of the usual bantering. He was serious and solicitous, putting a hand at the small of her back and steering her down the hall when she handed back the can.

"Are you ready to go down there? After you comb your hair and put lipstick on, of course."

"Let me get my purse and repair the damage." She recombed her hair quickly, adjusting the bow back to its original width. Meg wondered if the swipe of lip color did anything but accentuate the paleness of her face and the way the freckles stuck out.

She came out, running her hands down the skirt of her jumper. "Okay, let's do it. You coming down there?"

Alex nodded. He looked grim but determined. "I'll be right behind you, Maggie. Hang in there."

It was hard, but no harder than usual. Perhaps it

was even easier knowing that behind the range of the cameras and lights, away from the questions, she had a haven. Alex leaned against a wall, giving her a slow wink before she started making her statement. That alone almost made her lose her composure, but it was better than being nervous.

When it was over, Meg looked in his direction, but he wasn't there. Reporters clamored around her, pressing for more. "No, that's all I can say. No questions, please," she said, walking away from the lights. After a few minutes most of them gave up. A few stood talking to each other, and Meg knew that the two who had slipped out the emergency room door probably had headed for the precinct house to see if they could catch the arrest of the boyfriend.

Alex appeared from the hallway near the ER and put an arm around her shoulder. "Well, that's done. Let's get out of here."

"Fine with me. Let me go turn off the PC and tidy my office, then I'll be ready." Alex followed her upstairs. When the doors opened on her floor, Meg stepped out, only to run into a tall, thin blond woman.

"Janice, you shouldn't be up here," Alex said sharply.

"Yeah, well, neither should you. I really got all choked up there for a minute, thinking the lady had a knight in shining armor," the woman said. "Then I found out the guy they're arresting was a farm league player until this season. Just another story, right, Langdon?"

Meg whirled to face him only to discover he was

bearing down on the reporter, fury clouding his face. "I can't say let's not ruin a beautiful friendship, Janice, because we've never had one. But this is a new low even for you. Get out before I decide not to ask security to escort you out."

The woman smirked. "Sure. Keep it for yourself, then. I'll just go back to the station and tell Collins. He'll find it all very interesting."

"I'm sure he will, especially when he finds out about your cozies with the police dispatcher. Think he might object to what went on in the news van last week?" Alex shot back.

Janice's mouth dropped open, and the only image Meg had was of a fish, gasping for air. She still hadn't recovered when the doors of the elevator closed behind her.

The hallway was very quiet. "As God is my witness, Maggie, I have no idea who the guy is. However, if Janice says he's a minor league ball player, she's probably right. She may be obnoxious, but she's usually accurate."

Meg swallowed hard. The doubt had been momentary. She'd wondered why Alex had been so protective, and the thought that the reason had been a story had made her nausea return with a vengeance. But now it receded as she loosened her grasp on the papers she was holding and went to her desk.

She passed a notepad to Alex. "This is the man's name. I couldn't use it, not until the charges are filed. But if it rings bells . . ."

He passed it back, unread. "I'll have plenty of time to do this back at the station. I don't want you compromising yourself for me, Maggie." He broke into a slow, teasing grin, the first she'd seen all day. "At least, not that way."

She flipped the toggle switch on the computer. "Then walk me downstairs. I know you have to get going."

He shook his head. "Not yet. I'm getting in that car with you, and you are driving to the nearest grocery store. I am personally seeing to it that you get provisions to take home so that you will eat. And when I get back to your place after the ten P.M. news, I expect to find you in a fuzzy robe and slippers with a full report of a restful evening. Got it?"

"Yes, mother." She leaned up against him as they walked down the hall. "Do chocolate-covered raisins count as nutritional stuff?"

"Knowing you, they'll be a necessity. But we're buying some vegetable soup, too, Margaret."

"You really know how to spoil an evening, Alex."

Meg watched the news on KTIX, dutifully snuggled in her robe. Janice was strident and forceful. Somehow she'd managed to get shots of the mother, the boyfriend, and the police station. Alex was quiet and direct. The man *had* been a ball player, whose career had ended with injury and suspicion of drug use. It was not a pretty story no matter how it was reported.

The news had only been off ten minutes when Meg's doorbell rang. Meg always wondered at the way Alex filled a room when he came in. He stood still for a moment, looking around. "The ice cream is gone already, isn't it? An entire pint of rum raisin, and it's history."

"How can you tell? You can't smell ice cream."

"Yeah, and I can't smell soup either, Mutt."

"I was waiting for you. You used your break at the hospital with me instead of having dinner, so I figured you'd want something to eat." She walked smugly into the galley kitchen and turned on the stove burner under the soup and brought grilled cheese sandwiches out of the oven, where they'd been warming. "So there."

"I'm touched. Let me wash up and shed the tie."

In a few moments they had mugs of soup and a plate of sandwiches arranged near the easy chair and hassock they'd pushed together. A movie played on the VCR. "Pulled it out of my collection just for you," Meg said, watching Kevin Costner build a baseball field in his cornfield.

She leaned in closer to Alex, savoring the comfortable feel of his long legs on either side of her on the hassock. Alarm bells should have been going off in her head, with Alex this close, this late at night, alone. Instead, somehow there was a warmth around her. This was the way life was supposed to be. She settled in to enjoy it.

In the midst of a warm haze brought on by hot soup, crunchy crumbs of grilled cheese, and Alex surrounding her, Meg was nearly purring. "Hey, Langdon. You really come by just to protect me from Janice?"

"Sure did. But don't think it's going to become a

habit or anything. I just figured I owed you one after Saturday.''

Somehow the lazy way he stroked her hair belied the casual tone of his statement. Meg leaned back up against him. "My hero."

"Yeah?"

"Yeah. I know that's hard for you, not believing in that sort of thing."

He motioned toward the screen. "Now that's not true. Everybody ought to have heroes. I even have a few myself, somewhere. None of them would come out of a cornfield, but I have them."

Meg was feeling defiant as she picked up her soup. "Name three."

"I will, but not here and now. It's too late." He leaned back and squinted those bright blue eyes slightly. "I think I feel a column coming on. Give me a while here, okay?"

"Alex, if you keep running that hand around my, uh, collarbone, I'll give you all night. Willingly."

"Willingly?" Meg could actually watch his eyes change color, going gray-blue like the bottom of a clear lake.

Her tongue suddenly cleaved to the roof of her mouth. "Yep." It was all she could force out, looking at him.

"I'm not drunk tonight, Maggie."

"Neither am I." Her voice was coming out just a little shaky. "Sober as a judge."

Alex's skillful hand kept caressing her collarbone, dipping in larger circles each time. His intensity was driving Meg wild. "I keep thinking I'm going to find a flannel nightie if I prospect long enough here."

"It's April, Alex. Besides, I've outgrown flannel." Watching him, Meg felt terribly brazen. This was really the man she loved, staring at her with a yearning on his face that was unbelievable. Meg shrugged her shoulders and the robe slipped, revealing the straps of the satin chemise. She could see reflections of its gunmetal sheen in Alex's eyes, feel his intake of breath.

"Don't do this to me, Maggie. Not unless you mean it."

Meg could feel a smile starting at one corner of her mouth and a wellspring of feelings opening up inside of her. "What if I do?"

His answer was a line of wet, hot kisses that started at her naked shoulder and went up to the delicate skin just below her ear. Meg arched her back, bringing her into contact with his chest. In response, his hand slid across the smooth fabric of her gown to caress the blunt point of her breast. A moan escaped him as her nipple hardened with his touch.

Devouring her neck, Alex pulled her onto his lap, where Meg could feel the evidence of the passion she'd aroused in him so quickly. It gave her a feeling of triumph that Alex was as excited by her as she was by him. The contact gave Meg a sense of finality that sent a tiny thrill through her spine. There was still so much to tell him.

"Alex . . . I don't . . . I'm not prepared for this." The words were coming in ragged little bunches as he turned her gently in his lap to face him. His smile was slow and wolfish.

"Ah, Maggie, you forget, you're talking to a former Boy Scout. Be prepared is our motto." He grinned. "Even though since Trudi, I suspect most Boy Scouts have more reason to be prepared. I may be real rusty."

Somehow the admission endeared him to her like nothing else could. The truth of it shone in his eyes as he took in the smooth skin he was stroking, watched her rise in his lap to keep his hands moving over her body.

Meg leaned her forehead against his to whisper close to him. "At least you know enough to know you'll be rusty, Alex."

His eyes widened. "You're telling me you're not prepared because you . . ."

"Haven't ever had any reason to be prepared before."

His eyes clouded. "And you want me . . . ah, Maggie, you're too sweet."

Meg's throat was too dry to say anything. Too many emotions were warring while Alex's hands roamed her back. In answer she leaned down and kissed him, searching his mobile mouth with hers while her hands found the buttons of his shirt.

His chest was as magnificent as she'd remembered from Saturday night. With only the fabric of the chemise between them the heat from their bodies was overwhelming. Meg pressed Alex to her, still giving and taking in the sweet agony of his kisses, deep and searching.

Alex's breath was ragged when he pulled away

from her mouth at last. "This is a comfortable chair, Maggie, but no chair is comfortable enough for what I want to do."

"What *we* want to do, Alex," Meg said softly. In one fluid movement he picked her up and stood, swinging her high into his arms, and walked down the short hall to her bedroom.

He nudged the door open and set her down on the bed, struggling out of his shirt. For a moment Meg just sat and watched, entranced by the sight of him. Then she slid off her robe the rest of the way and started to pull down one thin strap of her chemise.

"Oh, no, you don't." Alex stayed her hand. "This is as good as Christmas, and I want to unwrap this package."

"We'll exchange gifts," Meg said, unable to resist an impish smile. She tucked her feet under her and reached for the waistband of his slacks. The garment slid to the floor, and she ran her hands over his flanks, feeling the muscles under her fingers.

His briefs were red this time, and just as brief as before. "You have wonderful taste in underwear, Alex," she murmured, hooking her fingers through the narrow sides and sliding gently down while she buried her face into the sensitive skin of his belly. "Umm, and you just plain taste wonderful." Meg marveled at the smooth skin under her lips, and the clean, heavy masculine scent of him.

As she nuzzled, Alex groaned and twined his fingers through her hair. "You're going to have to slow down, Maggie. We have all night, sweetheart."

Meg's eyes were alight as she faced him. "Oh,

but after all these years, all these fantasies, Alex.
And the reality is even better than my fantasies.''

He slid down beside her on the bed, sliding the
straps of the chemise down. The silky garment
slipped off her body to puddle around her knees.
Alex seemed rendered speechless for a moment.
"You're not the only one with fantasies, Maggie."

Leaning down, he captured the point of one breast
in his mouth. Meg gasped at her swift reaction to his
searching lips and clever tongue. Every muscle in
her body seemed to be working together to bring her
body closer to him, feel the heat pouring off him all
around her.

The heat was like being in a sauna, making her
languorous but invigorated at the same time, raising
a light sheen on Meg's body as she caressed Alex.
The skin of his shoulders and back was like warm
velvet as his busy mouth sought the other breast,
then traced a line of honeyed fire down the center of
her body.

He was everywhere, and she could not get enough
of him to satisfy the feelings he'd awakened. It was
all so new and so powerful, yet with Alex so terribly
right that Meg found herself fighting tears for a moment. Later, when he began to turn away from her
to open the shiny packet he'd fished out of his pants
pocket, she coiled around him. "No, let me watch.
Let me help. I want to do everything."

Alex's smile was slow and sweet. "I certainly
won't argue with that, Maggie." He reached out and
stroked her hair, his hand moving down to the base
of her neck. There was a certain urgency to the way

he stroked as she completed her ministrations. His chuckle was deep, and with her body curled around his back, Meg could feel it. "You still stick your tongue out when you're concentrating on something."

"Well, this is a new experience. I want to do it right."

"You're doing it right." Alex's voice seemed a little strangled. "So right that you may get another chance to do it all again unless you remove those fingers, Maggie."

In a moment they were together, Alex poised above her, his eyes deep pools, flashing with concern. "I don't want to hurt you. You'll stop me if it hurts."

"If it hurts," Meg agreed, already moving to accommodate him, welcoming him past the tightness, past the little flash of pain she tried mightily to hide. She wanted so much to give everything to Alex that she couldn't take anything away by admitting to pain.

Beyond the pain was Alex and all the joy she felt being with him, being part of him. Beyond was something that looked like a shimmering rainbow when she closed her eyes and listened to him murmur her name in her ear as he clasped her back, melding them together.

Later, after Alex eased her against the pillows and lowered himself down on top of her, Meg began to feel the day catching up with her. Her arms and legs felt like molten lead, weighing her down into the mattress. Alex turned them both gently until they were facing each other on their sides, Meg's hand tangled in the golden mat on his chest, feeling his regular breathing. She wondered crazily how the whole universe had shrunk to fit that small space within his smile and the heart beating under her fingers.

That was when she dozed off. Meg woke with a small start sometime later, still curled next to Alex, hand still on his chest. She expected to see bright blue eyes looking at her in amusement, but instead he was asleep too.

"Hey." She nibbled small kisses on his chest and shoulder until he woke, slowly. "Tomorrow's a workday, Alex. You need to go home?"

One eye open, he grimaced. "I ought to. Feed the fish and all that." His arm closed possessively around her. "But I don't want to."

"I don't want you too, either, but I look wretched in the morning even when I've gotten a full complement of sleep. This is probably as good as it's going to get."

"Good enough for me," Alex said, stroking her skin in long sweeps from her back to her hip bone. "If you won't kick me out, I'll stay, Maggie."

"Me? Kick you out? Never. Want an alarm?"

Alex nuzzled into her neck. "What time's yours set for?"

"Six."

She could feel the groan smothered by her skin. "That's barbaric."

"So you can roll back over. I might even let you

sleep.'' She ran her fingers down his spine and lingered near the base for emphasis.

The sound that came from him at her touch was part satisfaction, part groan. ''I've created a monster.''

Meg couldn't resist the laugh that bubbled up. ''Don't worry, I'll let you recoup until dawn. Maybe even until after work tomorrow night. We can get some Chinese food, rent a couple of movies . . .''

She could feel the chuckle as it started in Alex's chest. ''Yeah, maybe we'll even watch some of them. You've got a deal.''

Before he dozed off, Alex kissed her softly on the hairline, the temple, the nose, and once, soft and lingering, on the mouth. ''Pleasant dreams, Maggie.''

''How could they be anything but, with you next to me? My hero.''

''Keep saying that. I need a column idea for Thursday.''

She swatted him on the rump softly and pulled the covers up around them both. All night she dreamed of cornfields, but instead of baseball players, there was a sportscaster in every one.

THE MORNING STAR   SECTION D
                COMMENTARY
               Alex Langdon
    The arrest of Jimmy Wayne Crosslin
this week was difficult for many sportswriters to take. As one said when he
turned away from a briefing at police

headquarters, "It makes it hard to have heroes, doesn't it?"

Heroes do not face charges of battering a toddler to death. Heroes do not have a record of arrests for drug dealing and expulsion from one's chosen career.

Heroes are the golden figures of whom dreams are made. We put them on pedestals, only to have them jump down, crumbling those pedestals into dust.

Thankfully, my heroes are still on their pedestals. I am not among those this morning taking a load of gravel to the mental dump. But then, I guess that's because I've chosen my heroes differently.

I didn't choose them for their professional status or their career highlights. None of my heroes has ever made a commercial. The only thing they've endorsed were checks, and precious few of those.

If I had to pick only one of them, I'd say my hero still lives in the small town where she took up housekeeping 31 years ago. She still gets up at 4:30 every morning. In the summer she uses those early hours to bake bread for neighbors and putter around in her garden before the children come.

She watches a gaggle of children all summer, because their parents must be elsewhere. She doesn't complain about the tracks on the linoleum or the broken branches on the apple tree. Her flowers fill grubby hands more often then crystal vases.

In the fall, when they go back to school, so does she. She gets up at 4:30 because she must be at the high school cafeteria to start fixing lunch for 400 people.

It was the only job a widow with little education could get, fifteen years ago. So she took it, and her son never went without a thing. The medical bills left from her husband's lingering illness were paid, and it was only when the boy was in college that he realized his mother had not had a succession of black winter coats, but just one.

His first paycheck went for a bright red one with a fur collar. It was returned the next day for a serviceable black number. "You see," the woman said, "there's this lady who's just started at the cafeteria. She's a widow, and her children need school shoes. I figured with the difference ..."

She's still making the difference. My mother, May Langdon, still gets up at 4:30 every morning. And she's still my hero.

So is Coach Burns. He was my hero long before I went out for his baseball team. Freshman year of high school I did anything I could to stay after school and watch practice.

Raymond Burns was the size of a Texas Longhorn and had about as much tact. When I tried out sophomore year, he wasn't long-winded.

"Langdon, you're not bad. I could put you on the team, and you'd play a few games. You'd sit out most of them, but you'd play some. And you'd hate me," he told me, a hand on my shoulder.

He told me he'd read my stuff in the school paper. "That's the kind of thing that's going to get you into college, son. Not playing ball."

Coming from a lesser man, that advice would have made me hate him for life. My slot on the team went to a skinny little freshman kid who was all arms and legs. Sometimes, watching him from the bleachers turned a knife in my gut.

But Coach Burns kept supporting me long after he cut me from his team. I'd get clippings of a game I'd reported on for the school newspaper, and he'd scrawl "Nice job" across them. The parts he really liked he underlined. They were few but sweet.

When I got a summer job the next year with the real newspaper in town, I discovered I already had a reference on file when I applied for work. It was from Ray Burns.

Years later, the first time I got the company box at a professional game, the tickets did not go to my buddies. Instead, a man stooped from leaning over thousands of high school batters sat next to me. He brought two of his players. One was a gangly freshman who sat in awe of Burns, and perhaps of me, saying not one word the entire game.

"He's a good fielder," Burns told me. "But you should see him in the chemistry lab. There he's magic. I'm thinking of cutting him from the team."

Coach Burns's cuts have been legendary. There is a neurosurgeon and the president of a bank. A third is mayor of the town where he, and the coach, both live. One of the highest honors I have ever earned was being cut from the team by Raymond Burns.

So I have my heroes. They are not heroic in the ways of the world. I guess that's why I can't feel too sorry for Jimmy Crosslin.

He tried, for a while, to be somebody's hero. He failed miserably. Maybe he ought to take pointers from a lady at Mercy Hospital.

She's one of my heroes. She had to clean up after Jimmy Crosslin. She sat with his girlfriend when the doctors brought her word that someone had beaten her daughter to death.

She had to find a way to tell a gaggle of reporters without invading anyone's privacy. And she had to watch as the morgue van drove away with a very small passenger. That is heroic. Painful, and we would all hope unnecessary, but heroic.

When incidents like the one surrounding Crosslin happen, there's always pedestals left to fill. Happily, there are always people to fill them, if you look in the right places.

It's just that most of us don't look in the right places. We look at the bright lights of stadiums instead of the light that flickers on in a country kitchen at 4:30 in the morning. And that is our mistake.

SIX

On Thursday Gabe was definitely feeling better. Meg was still trying to figure out how she felt. Since Tuesday night, she'd been in a funny, misty state in which nothing seemed to disturb her terribly. She was still smiling absentmindedly when Kim came into her office, brandishing Gabe's latest practical joke.

"This has to be your doing, somehow, Margaret. No one else would have given Gabriel a rubber snake to put in his bandages." She waved the very realistic little green and yellow body before she put it on Meg's desk.

"Not guilty," Meg said, not looking up from the job at hand. "But it's a great idea."

"Meg, what are you doing? Cutting back a little on your snacks? I've never seen anybody cut chocolate-covered raisins in half before."

"Not trying to cut back, just verifying that they're really raisins."

"Sure," Kim said, patting her on the shoulder. "How much vacation time you have stored up, honey?"

"No, really." Meg looked up for the first time at her bemused friend. "See, Alex was over here for more than an hour Tuesday night, hanging around my desk, keeping me company."

"That, of course, explains everything."

"It would if you knew Alex." Hero worship was great, but Meg knew it wouldn't stop Alex if he was determined. "There have been times in the past when I have been known to let him within striking distance of my candy jar without checking. Ever had a chocolate-covered chili pepper? How about grasshoppers?"

"Ugh. I think I get the drift."

Meg swept the handful of candy into her mouth and chewed thoughtfully. "He must really be reformed. These were all raisins." *Perhaps he was saving all of his tricks for other places*, she mused, her face coloring at the direction that thought led.

Kim brought her back to earth. "Well, at least that solves one of our problems. But what did you do to Gabe?"

Meg felt herself go pale. "Why, is he worse?"

"No, just driving everybody on my floor nuts. If we're ten minutes late with the meds, he goes looking for the cart so he gets everything on schedule. He has gone to therapy every day and done the nasty stuff without being urged. And, of course, this morning when Smith came to check his 'itching' skin graft, she found Mr. Snake. You're magic. What'd you do?"

"Can't tell you, not until Saturday. Ask me then, okay?"

Kim gave the snake a flip, turning it over on its limp yellow belly. "Sure. But whatever it is, keep it up. It's really working. Looks like you're a hero to more than one person."

"Oh, go dry up, Kimberly," Meg called to her friend's back as she headed for the elevator.

Gabe was unrepentant when she went to lecture him at lunchtime. His tray was devoid even of crumbs, and he inhaled the candy bar she brought before she got settled in her chair.

"Now, look, Gabe, I have kind of a reputation around here. It's nothing bad, but they do tend to look to me when practical jokes are played. And somehow this . . ." she dangled the rubber reptile, "has been earmarked as belonging to me. And can you guess who Nurse Harris is going to get back at when she gets a brilliant idea? Not the young man who will be going home soon, I can tell you that."

"They thought that was yours? Oh, boy, that's great. Dad uses them to keep rabbits out of the tomatoes. He would have killed me if he knew what I used it for. They really thought you did it?"

"Yes, Gabriel, they did. I sincerely hope you will tell them otherwise." Meg's grin won the battle over the stern look on her face, and she stifled a laugh. His pale hair felt clean and short when she ruffled it. "I mean, if you're going to implicate me, I want in on the jokes, okay?"

He grinned back. "Sure. You going to be here tomorrow when the . . . uh . . . meeting happens?"

"Wouldn't miss it."

"Oh, that's right, your honey's coming too, isn't he?"

She stood to leave. "My honey? Arrgh. You're hopeless. Once the therapy's over and you're up to par at home, I want to challenge you to a duel. Water balloons at thirty paces."

"Great. You'll remember, I'm a catcher."

"I may regret this," she said from the door.

"May?" was his only parting shot before he used the remote control to turn on the day game again. At least he'd been gentlemanly enough to turn it off when she'd come in the room.

She was shaking her head when she came to the nurses' station and Kim was sitting there, arms crossed. "Well?"

"Wasn't me, honest. I know I've done plenty of things around here, but truly, I did not give Gabe the rubber snake. If I had given him a rubber snake, I would have gotten one a size or two larger than that one, Harris. Who's afraid of a garter snake?"

"You're right. I should have thought of that. Oh, well, we still took up a little collection on the floor for your birthday present just a bit early," she said, pulling a bag out from under the desk.

Meg took it gingerly and swung it. Nothing ticked, rattled, or sloshed. She slid a hand inside the bag. Felt like a perfectly innocuous shirt. As nurses clustered around the station, she pulled it out and groaned. "Call Me Mutt," letters proclaimed across the front.

"Thanks, guys. I should really thank each and every one of you personally."

"No, turn it over," Kim said.

Meg did. "And I'll bite you on the leg," she read. Looking at the shirt, she had visions of wearing it for Alex. She had a pair of little lace-trimmed bikinis that were the same color as the sleeves. But there were too many people watching now to think of that, and she had to make an answer. "Now that's a new low, even for you guys."

"We thought you deserved it," someone on the edge of the group said. "He have anything to do with the show tomorrow?"

"Who and what?" Meg said with a sinking feeling in her stomach.

"The sports hunk, Alex. He coming in tomorrow with your hot tub buddy?"

Meg flushed. "Listen, I don't know how you guys found out about this, but it could mean my job, and worse."

Kim Harris' brow puckered. "Is it that big a secret? I think every nurse on the floor knows. Gabe didn't exactly tell us outright, but he and his folks have been talking about it for days."

Meg groaned. "It's that big a secret. How quickly can you call a meeting in the dayroom?"

By four o'clock Meg had briefed both shifts that had daytime contact with Gabe. "Remember, no one is coming to the hospital tomorrow. Masterson values his privacy, and we're going to keep it that way for him. No cameras, no autographs unless he offers, no nothing."

"Nuts," somebody said in the back of the room.

"I know, but think of Gabe. I'll bet everybody in this room has a patient just as sweet as him. And if this works out for him, we may be able to do more for each one of them," Meg said. "But if we blow it, the word will get out and nobody will want to cooperate with us."

She slipped her shoes off and leaned on the windowsill. "Do you think we ought to switch his room?" she asked Kim. She'd stayed, half in her role of floor supervisor, half as Meg's friend, to listen to her speech a second time.

"It wouldn't hurt. We could ask Liz if it would be a problem, only for the one day. I know that there's an empty next to the therapy room up on four."

Meg nodded. "Fine. Now I've got a long day ahead tomorrow, and I want it to be a nice long day. If it is, I'll come in Saturday to catch up on my paperwork and wear my lovely new shirt. Deal?"

"Deal, Mutt," they all chorused. She couldn't resist the face she made at them as she left.

She almost had to wear the shirt the next day. After four clothes changes, Meg was desperate. Nothing looked quite right to suit Alex, Gabe, and Mike all at the same time. She gave up trying, finally, and decided to just please herself.

The pale pink and green floral dress had bows at the sleeves and the back. The lace inset just above the bust matched the lace ribbon Meg tied her hair back with, framing her face in strawberry-blond curls. Tiny pink porcelain rose earrings were the final touch as she put on her makeup.

Naturally, the phone rang when she was halfway through with her mascara. "Hi, you. It's me. We still on?" Alex's voice was a comfort.

"Sure are. Gabe wouldn't miss it for the world. I bet he didn't sleep a wink."

"Come on, Meg. You told me he's a sixteen-year-old boy. They eat like horses and sleep like rocks. Or even eat rocks and sleep like horses, standing up. They're indestructible."

"Well, Gabe almost wasn't. You will be nice to him, understand?"

"Yes ma'am. Almost as nice as I'll be to you afterward." His voice was a purr.

"No, Alex, I'm serious. I want you on your best behavior."

"This kid must be something else to bring out the mother hen in you."

"He is. See you around ten. You doing all right, Alex? You sound funny."

"Fine. Never been better. I just love walking into buildings full of people in white coats and kids who look like they've just survived a war."

"You'll be okay. I'll even hold your hand if you want."

"Now there's a possibility. See you later. And Meg?"

"Yes?" She shifted to arrange the waistband of her panty hose.

"I'm really looking forward to tonight. Bye."

Meg had hung up the phone, put the rest of her mascara on, and walked into the kitchen before she realized she hadn't told Alex about the room change.

She dialed his number back. The machine answered. "Rats," she muttered, rummaging in the freezer for something edible. There had to be better breakfasts than frozen lasagna. She left her message, hoping he'd call in for it.

Grabbing her purse, Meg headed for the door. She'd go to work early, check in on Gabe, and have breakfast in the cafeteria. Their muffins were better than anything she could find here, and after she ate, she'd call the station and the newspaper to hunt down Alex.

It wasn't that easy. He'd just left the television station when she called there, leaving a message anyway. Ten minutes later he was in the newspaper office somewhere, but no one had any idea just where. She left the message there, too, and hoped that Alex would check in with somebody—his answering machine or any of his human message takers.

She was going to have to guess which entrance they'd come in and intercept them. Meg looked at her watch. She still had more than an hour until they'd show up, even if they were running on Alex time, fifteen minutes early. "This is going to work out just fine," she told herself.

"Just fine," Alex said, strolling through the lobby of the hospital. "I figured you knew where we were going; you thought I knew where we were going. We're a real pair of winners, Masterson.''

His companion grinned, eyes crinkling behind sunglasses. "Yeah, I know. Amazing they want us here, isn't it?''

Alex looked at Mike. He honestly seemed excited about this. It was fun to watch, and it almost took his mind off being in a hospital.

Funny how they all smelled the same. The lobby was cleaning supplies and carnations in a trapped, circulated air kind of atmosphere. Just the whiff of that smell began to bring back all the bad feelings he'd been dreading. It was hard to handle the little kids running around in their robes and slippers, knowing that this was as close as they'd gotten to fresh air for some time.

Little flashes had already started to come back to him from the bad times. He fingered the beeper clipped to his belt. It was good to have the security of it there, knowing that the answering service would feed back the fake message any time he pressed in the code. Then he could slip out of here with a perfect excuse. Even Maggie couldn't get too angry at him if duty called.

And that way she'd never have to know what a terrible coward he was. The other night in the emergency room he'd almost bolted. It had all closed in too fast, too hard. But he'd stayed, even though it had cost him a night of dreams no human should endure.

Still, for her it had been worth it. Alex could imagine her little triangular cat's face, all the freck-

les, and the smile she seemed to reserve just for him.
That led to the other wonderful things she'd been
reserving just for him the last few nights, and for a
moment Alex forgot he was in a hospital.

It had always been that way. Maggie was home
and security and warmth. Pushing her away, making
her the enemy hadn't ever worked. It just proved
how much he lied to himself when he told himself
he didn't need those things.

One week with all of Maggie was enough to admit
that he needed those things desperately. He needed
them wrapped in strawberry-blond hair and bright
eyes, a strong, compact body, and a quick mind.
And tonight at dinner he was going to get them for
good if he had to talk for hours or feed her cham-
pagne until she couldn't talk at all.

But for now he still had to be here, enduring Masterson's slightly wry grin at the perspiration that was
beginning to break out on his forehead.

Some of the panic must be showing, even behind
the dark shades he wore, matching Masterson's own.
Mike looked at him, hard. "You don't really have
to be here with me, pal. You could just go on back
to the station."

"No, I'm staying," Alex said. He marched over
to the desk in the middle of the lobby where a blue-
haired matron presided. "Excuse me. We're looking
for a patient, Gabriel Kincaid."

She looked in a massive green and white computer
printout. "Kincaid. Now let me see."

Her long, thin finger, the nail polished in deep
red, traced the line. While she looked, longer and

longer, the first flutter jumped in Alex's chest. No, it couldn't be. Even Mutt wouldn't sink that low, not now.

"Oh, *Kincaid*. I was spelling it wrong. Gabriel Kincaid, third floor. Room three twelve. Go over to the elevators and take any one on the right-hand side."

"Thank you." Alex looked at Masterson, wondering whether to say anything. He pushed the thought aside. The lady had found the boy's name and room number. Even Mutt wouldn't be able to pull off that elaborate a stunt.

Or would she? That PC on her desk seemed to be hooked into everything at the hospital. Perhaps she could tap into admitting and make up a fake patient. If she could do that, this could all be an elaborate hoax that he would have a hard time explaining gracefully to Mike.

Alex kept his worries to himself while he fiddled with the keys in his pocket and waited for the elevator. "Still time to back out," Masterson said, looking at him when the door opened.

Alex shook his head as the people streamed out. "Not a chance. You think I'm letting you get all the glory? Besides, I want to see how you handle this, you wimp."

The elevator door closed, leaving just the two of them inside. "Wimp? What do you mean?"

"Mr. Big Shot Ball Player. No cameras, no publicity, no nothing. And who's the guy with the video camera?"

Masterson looked sheepish. "I got to thinking.

This kid, for whatever reason, is really looking forward to this. So maybe he ought to have a record of it. As long as it's my video camera, I can control what goes on."

"And you can have a copy to salve your ego the next time you go into one of your hitting slumps." Alex felt his spirits lifting. He liked giving Masterson a hard time.

His friend grinned and stepped out onto the third floor. "It won't hurt any. You coming?"

The smell up here hadn't changed any in fourteen years either. Maybe it was a little different, but not enough to keep Alex from feeling a cold sweat, willing away the urge to shiver. It was antiseptic and lunch trays and strong floor cleaner. There were metallic sounds, the squeak of rubber soles on tile floors, the constant interruption of a female voice on the loudspeaker. Alex knew that most of the staff didn't even hear that voice unless it called their name, their number.

He heard it, just as clearly as he had when he was outgrowing his Converse high-tops and the rub of them was the only thing that kept him distracted from the larger pain of watching his father die by inches. Walking down the corridor, he expected to see him in one of the doorways.

By then he'd been gauntly thin, the plaid bathrobe able to wrap almost twice around him. Where had his father's bulk gone in those few months? His strength had withered virtually overnight. At the end he looked like a guttering candle. Every time Alex visited, his throat closed off and he was sure the hospital was a tomb he'd never get out of alive. He had, but his father never did. Alex watched him die, and each time he visited him, he went home and methodically destroyed something the way that visiting his father was methodically destroying him.

His mother never asked where the notebooks went, why he had so many library fines, what happened to his baseball card collection and the marbles he'd kept in a leather pouch. Somehow she knew to leave him alone.

Maggie was the only one who'd ever bridged the panic that even the thought of entering a hospital engendered in him. That wretched night in college when he'd screwed up his knee and made it to the ER, sweating buckets, she'd been there the entire time. She'd held his hand, cajoled him, told him jokes as risqué as he'd ever heard from her—the innocent—all in an effort to take his mind off where he was.

It had worked, too, for the most part. The nightmares had lasted only as long as the painkiller for the knee. Once he was off the drugs, the incident faded swiftly. Sweet Maggie, his charm against fear. For a moment Alex almost regretted not telling her about his fears. Where was she now?

"Three twelve," Masterson announced. He knocked on the partially open door, but nothing happened. He pushed it open and looked inside. "Weird. Nobody home."

"Maybe he's in the . . ."

"Nope. Door's open." He went inside the room

a step. "This is really strange, Alex. There's not even a *bed* in here."

The panic and the anger washed over him like a wave. Alex pushed away the urge to pound on the cinder block wall. This was not happening to him.

Masterson didn't seem able to see the panic that was making Alex's heart beat faster, constricting the collar around his neck. He walked past Alex, looking out into the hallway. "Maybe we can find someone who knows what's going on."

"I have a feeling there's only one person who knows, and she's laughing her guts out somewhere." His voice was so soft that Masterson didn't hear him as Alex joined him in the hall.

The only person in sight was a nurse coming out of the room next to them. No, it wasn't a nurse, it was an aide. This girl couldn't be more than a teen-ager in her crisp uniform. She nearly levitated when Alex spoke to her.

"Excuse me, miss. We're looking for Gabriel Kincaid's room."

She turned around, large brown eyes widening to amazing proportions. Her head whipped around as if she were looking for someone else, anybody to get her out of this predicament. "Gabriel Kincaid," she echoed, looking at them again.

"That's right. It's supposed to be three twelve, but . . ." Masterson said apologetically.

The girl looked at them again, and Alex got the impression of a doe ready to flee. "There's nobody here by that name, honest." She didn't wait to make any more explanations but took off down the hall and turned the corner at a rapid clip.

"What was that all about, I wonder?" Masterson pushed his sunglasses up on his head.

"I think I have an idea. This is a scam, my friend." Alex's throat was so tight he had to force his voice out.

"A scam?"

"Right. There is no Gabe, no poor little fellow languishing in a hospital bed. April Fools' just came late this year." The panic was fueling a colossal dose of anger. That, at least, was better than being so scared he wanted to turn and run.

"Not possible. Meg wouldn't do that to you again, Alex."

The panic was welling up, even stronger. The image he had of Maggie, made hoydenish by his attention, leaning over him, just didn't mesh with what was happening now. Still, it was happening. "Right. You know the little witch so well. This is just her revenge. Maybe there was some kid, or some good reason for her to look you up the first time, but take it from me, this is it, Michael." Alex looked down to see why his hand hurt and stopped banging it against the wall behind him, unclenching his fist.

"You're wrong. This is just some kind of foul-up. I'm going to look for the nurses' station. You coming?"

"Sure." He followed the ball player, feeling like a robot. Keep walking, head forward. Don't look into any of the rooms. Do not listen for muffled laughter. He was all right until they turned the corner and the room was right in his field of vision.

It was a dayroom of some kind. Sunlight streamed in, on the children playing, on the one in the corner banging on the battered piano. It was the girl doing the puzzle who did him in. She worked with the massive absorption of youth, unaware of the tied bow on her flowered pajama top coming unraveled, fitting in puzzle pieces with one hand, tongue out in concentration while her other hand scratched the nearly bald skull with tiny wisps of brown fuzz coming out in tufts.

The pain and the sorrow washed over him too fast, and Alex ran into the wall with his shoulder. There was a haze of feelings around him now, and none of them were good. Joke or no joke, there was no choice now. Maggie wasn't here to chase the panic that was enveloping him. He had to get out of here. Alex reached up to his belt, squeezing the beeper. Its strident nagging stopped Masterson in his tracks. ''That yours?''

The words all came out in a rush. ''Yeah, it is. Probably the station. I told them where I'd be if anything major came up. I'll catch up with you later maybe, okay?''

Masterson's expression asked questions that didn't make it to his lips. ''Fine. Take care, Alex.'' Mike seemed about to reach out to him as he turned, quickly, and went back to the elevator. Mercifully, it was swift and empty. In the lobby he noticed no one, saw not one soul in the six blocks he walked to the newspaper.

It was quieter here. No one was likely to bother him, especially not when he was in the tiny cubicle that held only his PC, desk, and chair. When Alex Langdon was here, he was on deadline and in solitary and no one stuck their head in.

It was just as well. Today he would have bitten it off. His feelings kept warring, tossing him from one emotion to the other. *What did the last few days mean if this was all a colossal joke? And if it wasn't, would Maggie ever want to see him again now that he'd run out on her? It had to be a joke,* he told himself. He could just picture Maggie, what she was telling Masterson, scoring another coup against stupid old Alex.

She'd always been the quick one, the bright, sure of herself young woman, never realizing how she comforted him or tantalized him with what she took for granted. And now, again, she'd taken his composure and destroyed it.

Alex laid his head in his hands, slumping down toward the desk. No, she had not destroyed him. He was the only one destroying anything. There probably was a Gabriel Kincaid someplace in that hospital. But there were also too many memories, too many fears.

Hating Maggie for a few minutes had given him a fine excuse to leave the hospital. But he couldn't keep it up for good. The love was creeping back, seeping into his bones as it had since he'd seen her in the depths of the stadium weeks ago.

He couldn't possibly love Maggie Shepherd. Not the way she deserved to be loved. After all, she liked

her job. Really liked it. No amount of explaining
was going to make her understand how he hated her
hospital and every other one. And knowing Maggie,
she'd offer to quit working there just to make him
feel better. Then she'd hate him afterward. There
was only one thing to do. Break things off nice and
clean, now, so that she could get on with the kind
of life she deserved. He could just take his memories
of the last few weeks and store them, a treasure
against the rest of his life, and let her get on with
hers.

Alex picked up the telephone to cancel the reserva-
tions they'd made at the expensive restaurant across
town, then put the receiver back in its cradle. No,
let her just show up. Knowing Maggie and her legendary temper, being stood up would keep her from
coming back to wonder what was going on.

The blank screen in front of Alex mocked him.
He was never at a loss for words, but this time was
different. This time he was watching all his renewed
hopes and dreams go into meltdown. The only column he wanted to write would have a very limited
audience.

After ten more minutes with nothing productive
happening, he gave up. He slipped a diskette in the
machine and pulled his evergreen column on umpires
he'd been saving for a rainy day. He transferred it
down to the desk and sat back.

"All right, let's get down to business," Alex muttered to himself. Why not? He'd write it, he'd print
it out, he'd have it delivered. If only there were
judges for this sort of thing, it would probably win

a Pulitzer. He didn't think they had a Dear John/ Dear Jane letter category, though.

An hour later Alex was satisfied. He picked up the phone and punched in some familiar numbers. "Bill? Alex Langdon. I need something special. What have you got in the way of carp?"

SEVEN

The aide flew into the room and stopped in front of Meg's desk. "You were right, Ms. Shepherd. There were reporters looking for Gabe."

Meg's temper flared as she stood up. "What did you do?"

"I told them there wasn't anybody by that name. They were looking in his room."

"And then?"

"And then I came up here. I figured they'd find Kim."

"She can handle them," Meg said. "Let's go see what's happening."

Alex was going to kill her if anybody found Gabe's real room. Meg thanked her lucky stars that she had the foresight to move him. But now she had a real problem. It was about time to start looking for Alex and Masterson. If she did that, she might lead the reporters right to them.

She turned to the aide as they waited for the elevator. "What did this bunch look like?"

"Two guys, one carrying a video camera. Both kind of good-looking," she said, with a little giggle.

"Aren't they all?" Meg said. Bunch of charming suckers, just like Alex. No, Alex was the most charming, and the most aggravating. He would never appreciate the lengths she'd gone to protecting their agreement.

The teenager mused while she watched the numbers flash in the elevator. "I thought they dressed better than that, though. Both these guys were in jeans."

Both of them? Meg's head swung around quickly. "What did they look like? Describe them, physically."

"The one with the camera was a blond, really tight jeans. The other guy had darker hair and was real tall. I think I've seen him someplace before."

Meg nearly launched herself out of the elevator when it opened on the third floor. "We may have just saved Mike Masterson from himself," she told the surprised girl as they headed for the nurses' station.

Kim Harris wasn't there, and no one was positive where she had gone. Some said to security, some said up to Gabe's room. Meg found the staircase and hopped up the stairs two at a time. She was winded when she pushed open the door to the fourth floor, and there was a pounding in her ears.

Over the pounding she could hear laughter and commotion coming from Gabe's new room. When she looked in, Kim Harris and Spence Kincaid each had a hand on Mike Masterson's shoulder, laughing.

Gabe stood watching the trio, beaming while Martha tried to operate the video camera.

Gabe's mother clucked as she aimed the camera at her grinning husband. "Now if you all have your heads cut off, don't blame me. I've never been good at these things."

Meg leaned against the door frame in relief. Plunging up the stairs she had envisioned it all going awry. Only one thing was missing. Alex wasn't in the room.

She'd expected to see him lounging in one of the chairs or directing the show somehow. Instead, there seemed to be a gaping hole in the fabric of the little scene before her.

Masterson spotted her and waved. "You run a tight ship, Meg. I had to show the dragon lady here my driver's license before she'd believe who I was."

The brown skin around Kim's deeper brown eyes crinkled as she smiled. "So you look different out of uniform. And I didn't expect you to be looking like the enemy," she gestured toward the camera. "I hope that thing is off."

"It is," Martha said. "I think somebody else needs to do this."

They taped all kinds of silly things in the next half hour. There was Gabe with Mike, Spence with Mike, Mike kissing Martha (who blushed beautifully), and variations on all of it. Once they all sat down with cold soft drinks, Meg was able to be casual. "Where's Alex, anyway?"

Mike's answering look was a little odd but passed

quickly. "His beeper went off downstairs. He didn't even make it up here."

"Typical Alex. Think it was legitimate?"

"What do you mean?"

"I mean, knowing Alex, he may have arranged that little distraction to keep from hanging around."

"Could be. He about had a stroke when that little nurse's aide told us Gabe didn't exist."

"I'll bet. But he was the one who said security had to be so tight that nobody could slip through. And he was the one who gave me the idea that somebody might try something like that. I'll have to give him a hard time over dinner."

"Give him one for me while you're at it," Mike said, smiling. "I think I owe him one or two."

"Will do." Meg stood up and ruffled Gabe's hair. "I'll leave you guys alone. Have a good time."

Gabe's smile was radiant. "We will. Thanks, Meg." He reached for her hand and gave it a hard squeeze.

Meg left the room feeling as if she were walking on a cloud. Not even Alex's pooping out on her could ruin this feeling. Gabe had his dream, and she had a part in making it work. This was heaven.

She went back to her desk, trying to sort through all the projects that had been pushed aside yesterday while she had tightened the security around Gabriel. It was after noon when she was aware that necks were craning around the office, and a dashing young man stood in front of her, smiling.

"Well?"

"Well, what?" Mike's grin was infectious.

"You said I could buy you lunch after I finished upstairs. I had to go. I felt like I was wearing Gabe out."

"I did say that, didn't I?" She reached into her bottom desk drawer and retrieved her purse. "You sure you want to do this? The rumor mills around this place are excellent. Your presence in that cafeteria will be known once you put one foot inside."

He shook his head. "That's all right. Today I don't mind it, I'm going to have a lot to talk about with Alex. It seems we're both going to have to break our promises."

Meg tried not to blush. "If you're ready for this, so am I. Should be fun. I don't often get to nibble fish sticks with a celebrity."

It was Masterson's turn to blush. Meg liked the way the back of his neck, tanned above the collar of his shirt from spring training, turned deep pink. She idly wondered if Alex would consider asking him to be best man.

The implications of that thought slammed her against a wall mentally. She had no business making any plans that included Alex Langdon. Once, in girlish dreams, she'd done just that and gotten shot down. Even though the chemistry was there between them, there was no reason to believe anything would ever come of it.

Alex was an ambitious dreamer, and those dreams meant more to him than she ever could or would. There would be no wedding party to choose, no ceremonies to plan. So those honeymoon suite fantasies would have to be banished as well. There just wasn't any place for them in the real world, not one inhabited by the real Alex Langdon.

Granted, she loved him. Meg knew now that whatever happened in her life, she'd continue to love Alex. But love and forever didn't seem to be words that went together in the Langdon dictionary the way they did in hers.

"Earth to Meg." Mike's hand waved slowly in front of her face. "Where you been, lady? Looks like you sleepwalked your way down here. Lucky for me you can find the cafeteria even on automatic pilot."

Meg shook herself out of her thoughts, sheepishly. "Yeah, I can. Sorry about that, Michael. Grab a tray and I'll lend you a pen. Looks like the autograph hounds are descending."

Mike did get to finish his salad, somehow, between all the visitors. Nurses came over in gaggles. Interns shook his hand and clapped him on the shoulder. Liz came over, in scrubs as usual, and made her own introductions.

"I just popped up to see Gabe. You've done wonderful things with him. I've thought about writing you up in a medical journal," she told him.

Mike blushed even deeper than Meg had seen him before, and to Meg's amazement, he traded phone numbers with Liz in case she wanted to talk about Gabe some more. She left to get a quick lunch as Meg looked at both of them in surprise. Her standoffish friend and Alex's hermit buddy had just traded phone numbers. And across the cafeteria Liz actually flashed her some kind of victory sign while Mike grinned like a teenager.

"All right, Michael," she tried to admonish. It wasn't doing any good. In a controlled setting like this, Masterson seemed to be enjoying the attention. Especially Liz's attention. He seemed to be disappointed that she had to take her lunch and go elsewhere.

Meg didn't blame him. It had to be a strange kind of life, training, practicing, pitching, and traveling. "So was this fun after all?" she asked between admirers.

He leaned back in the orange plastic chair and stretched. "It was. I really got a kick out of Gabe, Meg. Thanks. I told him that when he's well enough to get out of here I expect to see him at the ballpark. When I get back, I'm going to leave his name at the front office for the box some time in May. He'll be out then, won't he?"

His face looked serious for a minute, and Meg was struck with the knowledge that he really did care. "Yes, we hope so. This week has been unbelievable. Once he knew you were coming he went from a draggy, feverish kid to a ball of energy. His skin graft is taking, and he should walk out of here on his own in about two weeks."

"That's fantastic. It really did make a difference, huh?"

Meg crushed her milk carton and gathered up her trash. "Mike, you saw that bunch of pictures on his wall. That wasn't done for your benefit. In fact, when we moved his room this morning, he insisted they had to come along, even if he was going to be up there just for half a day. When he moves again this afternoon, they'll go with him. You're his hero."

Masterson was blushing again. "Oh, come off it," she said. "Surely you know that kids are going to idolize you. From their perspective, you've got the perfect job, and you do it well."

"I guess I do." His voice was slow, thoughtful. "There are others out there, like Gabe, aren't there?"

"Sure are. Kim Harris has another little one on her floor, a girl. She's got pictures of Mickey Mouse up like Gabe has yours. All she wants to do is shake his hand once. Of course, that might be a little difficult to do until she gets a prosthesis, but she intends to do it anyway. Unfortunately, her dad got laid off last month, and her mother has been out of work for a year caring for her."

"I get the idea. Think we could do anything about that?"

"What's this 'we' stuff, kemosabe? I've already got a full-time job in this place," Meg chided. Masterson stood up, reaching for his tray, and she did the same.

"Yeah, well, I guess it deserves some thought."

It apparently deserved a lot of thought, starting immediately, because Mike was quiet as she walked him to the parking garage. When they got to the car, Meg hugged him on impulse. He squeezed her back. "Thanks, Meg. I needed this."

"Gabe did too. Take care of yourself, okay. How hard a time should I give Alex for you?"

"Only moderate. I may need a favor from him soon."

Meg tilted her head slightly, trying to figure that one out. "Okay, fine. See you."

He got into his car and drove away, and Meg went back to her office. Only a few hours to wade through all this paperwork before she had dinner with Alex.

Five thirty rolled around very fast. Meg swept the piles of paper still left on the desk into some sort of order and dashed into the ladies' room. She took down her hair and started over, adding a spritz of cologne as she did so. After tying the bow back into some sort of order, she went to work on her face. In a few moments she was satisfied.

"This is only a dinner date, after all," she told the reflection in the mirror, now sporting a few less freckles and a little more color. "Hey, a dinner date with Alex and he didn't even make me sign a release. Cool."

As she left the garage, something on the dash caught her eye. "Oh, Baby, what a time to be a nag," she told the car. Timing or not, the little light that went on when the fuel got way under a quarter of a tank was flashing on and off.

She pulled into the first station that would take her credit card and pumped a tank full of gas. Then she washed her hands to get the nasty smell off and raced back to the car.

Gathering her skirts in so she didn't slam them in the door, it happened. Her leg grazed the edge of the door, and she felt a ladder climb all the way up her leg. Looking down confirmed it; there was a gaping run from her ankle on up. "Damn. Can't I do anything right tonight?"

Naturally, the convenience mart at the gas station didn't have any panty hose. The drugstore two blocks down did, but there was no place to put them on. The fast-food place three blocks closer to the restaurant where Alex was probably fuming by now looked like a welcome haven, filled with people on their way home and teenagers with huge radios. Meg slipped into a stall and put on the new hose. Now she was ready to go again.

It was well after six when she got to the restaurant, gave the car to the valet, and hurried in. She expected to see Alex in the lounge, jacket off, tie askew, and fire in his eye. He hated to be kept waiting, even though he was perpetually early.

The lounge was full, but no Alex. When Meg talked to the maître d', he confirmed that, yes, Mr. Langdon's reservation had been made, but no one was at the table. "However, if you'd care to wait there, I can relay any messages."

After the last hour, Meg felt frazzled. "Please."

The dining room was more elegant than the hotel where they'd had lunch weeks earlier. Meg looked around at the pearl-gray walls and upholstery, the white linens, the shimmering candles in crystal holders and relaxed a little. She ordered an iced tea and sat back to wait for Alex.

It gave her a little smug pleasure to be there first for a change. That was a real rarity. She could think of it happening only a few times in all the years she'd known him. Alex had always been the proverbial young man in a hurry. What was he hurrying after, really? And would he ever slow down long enough for someone to go with him? Again Meg wished that she could be the one to slow him down, just to a trot. That pace would let her keep up with those long legs for the journey.

"Would you care for me to refill that?" The waiter at her elbow startled her. She looked at the empty goblet, than at her watch. Six thirty and still no Alex.

"Please. And could you tell me where the telephone is?"

The waiter pointed it out, and Meg started fishing for quarters. Ten minutes later she was seventy-five cents poorer and no wiser. Alex didn't seem to be anywhere, according to her calls. The station hadn't sent him out on assignment, nor had anyone seen him recently, the sports desk at the paper professed ignorance; and his home phone was on the machine. A total blank.

Meg went back to the table, expecting him to be sitting there by now, laughing at her concern. Still, the chair was empty, mocking her. As she sat down, smiling weakly while the waiter refilled her glass of tea again, she was uneasy.

It was time to either start calling hospitals or decide that she'd been had. There were only two possibilities here. Either Alex had been detained by some terrible accident, or he *was* a terrible accident. The second choice was beginning to look more and more likely.

Meg squeezed a fresh lemon slice into her tea, rattling the ice cubes idly. Surely even Alex wouldn't be rude enough to strand her in a first-class restaurant like this as a joke. *Not unless this was just the punch line*, she thought to herself. Alex could only do that if the last few weeks had been his idea of the sweetest possible revenge.

Perhaps the column he wrote in the beginning had been only half the story. Perhaps Alex hadn't really felt they were even until now, when he could picture her sitting here like an idiot.

Meg looked at her watch again. It was almost seven. Not even Alex would have been this late on purpose. She put enough money to cover the tea and a tip on the table and left, ignoring the stares she knew were following her out the dining room. Why didn't she just put a big sign on her back that said "Stood up?"

The car started flawlessly, no parts of her apparel got caught in anything, and she made it home in record time. Going up the stairs to her apartment, she was sure she heard the telephone ringing upstairs, so she hurried. Just past the landing, the ringing stopped. But propped against the door was a long rectangular white box with a crisp green ribbon. It looked like an expensive apology, and Meg lunged to get it quickly before it disappeared.

It was getting dark in the apartment. Meg noticed that she could barely make out the outline of the white box lid anymore. The bottom of the box was safely in the dumpster downstairs. She'd ruined the new pair of nylons kicking the metal container, but it was worth it.

A dead fish. Alex had sent her a dead fish and a terrible letter. She switched on the lamp next to her favorite chair, making a little pool of light in the gloom. She ran one tired finger down the lines of print. It looked just like his newspaper column, only printed out from his computer, in the same typeface as her morning paper.

Alex had never been this nasty in his column in the paper though, not to anybody. Here was a biting sarcasm that hit the mark and brought tears to her eyes. This just wasn't Alex, not the Alex she knew and loved.

The thought stopped her stock-still. *This wasn't Alex.* Sure, he'd written this. But the last few weeks hadn't been a practical joke. Meg knew in her heart that Alex had been real. This wasn't the end of a beautiful friendship either. Alex might say he was tired of the chase, but that was a smoke screen.

The trouble was, could she figure out what the smoke was screening? Meg sat in the dark and pondered. Alex had taken off like a shot this morning. He wasn't dumb enough to think that Gabe had been an invention, not really. So why did he set off his own beeper, as Meg was sure now that he had?

The phony newspaper column in her hand was getting uncomfortable and she set it on the floor. It began to nag at her though, not something she'd read in this column, but something else she'd read. Beside the chair was the stack of sports sections she'd begun to save, all folded to Alex's columns.

She switched the light on and began to read. In a few moments she had it. It was the column he'd written about heroes. His father had died when he was a teenager. Cancer, she remembered from college. But that was all she remembered. Alex never talked about it, never went into detail.

Meg leaned back in her chair, paper in her lap. She could see an image of Alex in her mind. Alex tense and drawn with pain, Alex pale and shaky. Alex in the emergency room getting a knee x-rayed, and obviously so scared he could barely sit still. In her memory, only the immobility required by the knee kept him from flying out of there.

Was Alex phobic about hospitals? Was this whole silly thing about tile walls and antiseptic? There was only one way to find out. Meg put down the newspaper and picked up the phone, dialing information in Muncie, Indiana.

Two calls later she had a woman with a soft, sweet voice on the other end of the line. "Hi, May? This is Meg Shepherd. You may think this is a stupid question. . . ."

Her long-distance bill was going to be a dandy. Meg put the phone back on its cradle and stood up. "You're not going to get away with this, Langdon. Not this time. No riding off into the sunset, pardner." In a moment she was out of the room and into her bedroom, kicking off pumps, shedding the dress. It was cute, but nothing to wear when one declared war.

The black jeans were kind of snug, but they were undoubtedly the item in her wardrobe least like anything from her college days, especially when paired with the sweater that dipped precipitously in front and even lower in the back. Heels gave her the possibility of coming higher than Alex's breastbone. Maybe she'd have a few more negotiating points if he could see her face.

The security guard at the front desk at KTIX was less gullible than the day receptionist but just as familiar with Alex. "Yeah, he's in there. Had a pizza delivered on his break. Didn't even go out."

After a bit of wrangling, he let her into the station. If he hadn't been a reader, it might have been more difficult, but once Meg proved that she was the infamous victim of the locker room joke, the guard waved her through. He didn't even take her up on her offer of a search through her purse to prove no weapons were involved. Meg wondered how many other people had been Alex Langdon practical joke victims. Maybe they could start a support group.

The pizza box was still on his desk, mostly full. One slice was gone, and Meg could see most of it peeking out of a napkin in the trash. It gave her a vague satisfaction that Alex didn't seem to have any appetite either.

What gave her very little satisfaction was that he didn't appear to be around. She wished he had given her the full tour of the station before. Then she'd know where he was. Footsteps in the hall made her turn around just as he came through the doorway.

"What the hell are you doing here?"

"Don't worry, I'm not returning your fish. That

got shoved in the dumpster. That sucker was really ripe, Alex.''

"You deserved it." His eyes blazed with a bitterness that nearly made her wince.

"No, you *thought* I deserved it," Meg said, coming up and planting a finger on his chest. She pushed away the feelings that rose from touching him. "Now you are going to show me where the tape equipment is in this station, mister, and you are going to do it quickly."

Five minutes later, Alex was sitting on the edge of a desk, watching Gabe and Masterson joke around on the screen in front of him. "See what you missed, Alex?" Meg said softly.

"Yeah, well, my beeper went off."

"Right. And I know exactly why. I called your mother, Alex. This time, you're not getting away with it. No blowing the smoke off the six-shooter and kissing your horse, Alex. This time you stay and talk it out." Meg faced him, and he pulled his gaze from the screen to look at her.

His eyes were incredibly blue, so deep she wanted to float in them. There was confusion there and a little bit of pain. "What if I don't want to?"

"Then I'd have to use one of Gabe's phrases and call you a real dork," Meg said. "But that would be maligning the man I love."

"Love?"

"Even after this stunt, Alex. That's why I'm not going to let you get away with it."

"You're going to forgive me this easily?" One corner of his mouth curled up as his hands slipped around her waist. Meg neither pulled back nor walked into his embrace but just stood there.

"Easy? Mister, I guarantee this will be the hardest thing you've ever done."

"No, walking into that hospital this morning was the hardest thing." He nuzzled into her hair, so carefully arranged less than an hour before to try to give her a more sophisticated air. So much for that.

"So far. Stick around and it will get harder. I do love you, Alex, but I'm not going to spend my life second-guessing you or protecting you from life's little disappointments. If you want me to know something, you'll have to tell me about it. And if you're angry about something, I want to know in words, not deceased marine biology. Got it?"

Alex sighed. "Got it." He returned to nuzzling her hair, and his hands planted themselves more firmly on her waist. Meg resisted a shiver as her hands found his shoulders, tracing a smooth path up his smooth broadcloth shirt, feeling the taut muscles underneath.

"Well, if you've got it, keep listening. Lovers do not give people rose boxes with corpses in them. Lovers do not blow petty misunderstandings into World War Three."

"Lovers spend time in each other's offices eating pizza and making out," he murmured into her hair.

When she pulled back in surprise, she could see the delight dancing in his eyes. "Hey, it was worth a try. I'm starved all of a sudden. And pizza sounds good, too."

"Okay. Let me get the tape out of the player. And

I expect you to make copies of this. One for me, and one for Michael.''

"Michael? You call him Michael? Hoo, boy.''

Meg waggled a finger at him as they walked down the hall. "Don't hoot like that. He's very nice. And for whatever reason, he thinks you're a prince of a fellow. You ought to be flattered.''

"I ought to be jealous. He spent the whole morning with you and I didn't.''

"Nobody's fault but your own. That beeper call really was a phony, wasn't it?''

"That look is priceless, Maggie. I feel like I'm being quizzed by my sixth-grade teacher. And she wore a habit.'' Alex sighed. "Yes, Maggie, it was fake. Is this the end of True Confessions?''

She turned on the light in his office. "Not quite. Sit down.''

He sat. Meg stood in front of him, longing to go back to tracing patterns on his shoulders, finding his mouth. It would have to wait. "I'm not leaving just because hospitals give you the willies, Alex.''

"Not leaving me, or not leaving the hospital?'' There was a challenge in the depth of his eyes.

"Not leaving either. So where does that leave us?''

"You tell me,'' he said, pulling her to him. His kiss started out gently, but the hunger was hard to control. Only when Meg was dying for air did he let her go. "Well?''

She was trembling. "It definitely leaves us somewhere, doesn't it?''

"I'd say so." Alex seemed to be having almost as much trouble as she was getting enough air.

Meg squared her shoulders, trying to be serious. "In that case, there are going to be some ground rules. One, we really talk."

He trailed several small, very hot kisses up from her collarbone to her neck. "We talk. Agreed."

"Two, I want some normal dates. I want to be courted, Alex."

"Does this mean I have to send live flowers?" His voice was low and husky in her ear.

Her hands were tangling in his hair. Slim, responsive fingers were underneath her sweater, counting her ribs from the back. "Real live flowers. I had a third condition, but it's . . . slipping my mind."

His chuckle before he claimed her mouth was deep. "Don't worry. Anytime it comes to mind, you speak right up. I'm all . . . ears."

Meg slid her hands down from his belt to verify what she already knew. "Among other things."

There was a groan deep in his throat as he devoured her mouth. She could feel it rumbling in his chest when she put a hand there. Alex trapped the hand there when he drew her to him. Pressed there, she could feel both of their hearts racing as his tongue plundered. Her answering touch of the inside of his mouth made his heart race even faster.

He was actually panting when he forced her, gently, away from him. "Damn, Maggie. Honey, I've got to go back to the newsroom while I still can. Wait here, all right?"

"All right." She pushed her hair back from her face, feeling the flush he'd left on her skin.

Later, she decided she should have one of the engineers dub the tape of that particular sportscast onto the end of her copy of Gabe and Masterson.

Never had Alex looked quite so bemused. Or quite so glad he was sitting down behind a high desk. She wanted to keep the sight for posterity.

THE MORNING STAR   SECTION D
                    COMMENTARY
                  Alex Langdon

There are jokes, and then there are jokes. My friends (and some people who will term themselves former friends) will tell you that I enjoy a good joke in almost any form, even when it's on me. Well, almost always when it's on me.

There are jokes of the practical nature, like the Cubs, and then there are jokes of the cosmic nature. A cosmic joke makes one believe that someone larger than you and me is rocking back on his or her celestial heels and laughing. Hard.

One of those cosmic jokes happened to Gabriel Kincaid. Actually, his set off a whole string of them, like firecrackers, but I'm getting ahead of myself. One moment he was watching his cousin drive a tractor. The next minute the tractor was heeling over on top of his cousin and Gabe was using the muscles and reflexes developed in eight seasons of baseball to push his cousin out of the way. Then the tractor was down. On top of Gabe.

Nasty stuff happens next. There's ambulance rides and traction and debridement (a form of medieval torture adapted for use on burn victims), which means Gabe spends a good chunk of his junior year of high school in situations a whole lot less fun than the junior prom.

Through all of this, Gabe remained philosophical. I caught up with him the other day at Mercy Hospital. He said yeah, he'd do it again, even if it meant he wouldn't play ball.

Now this is akin to the rest of us saying we'd do it again if it meant we wouldn't breathe anymore, according to his folks. Their home, a farmhouse between Washington and Union, is full of baseball stuff, just like the space over Gabe's hospital bed. In the living room are Little League trophies, high school pictures, and framed jerseys from winning state teams. Gabe's collection had a different theme.

Above his bed is the Bat Masterson Hall of Fame. And despite what I have said a few times, the folks at Mercy got the idea that maybe the Batman would come and talk to his number one fan.

Enter cosmic joke number one. Masterson actually did it. As a result, the kid who by all rights should be taking up basket weaving is instead going to be back at catcher later this season. He's also got a brand new friend.

His brand new friend is getting him into the Cardinals' physical therapy program when he walks out of the hospital next week. And into the team box for a game or two. And possibly onto the playing field itself. Gabe can't say enough about Masterson.

"The first couple of weeks, I asked myself what I was doing here. Why didn't I just give up? Now I know, I guess," Gabe says, softening up a glove he's really going to use again.

Masterson knows, too. He says it isn't about one kid in a hospital bed, however heroic. Enter cosmic joke number two. The man who has spent three years avoiding publicity has decided to create a foundation and become its spokesperson.

Starting today, Mercy Hospital, along with my newspaper and Masterson's ball team, is sponsoring something called "Mike's Make-a-Dream-Come True." The fund will benefit kids with a terminal illness, or a serious problem that isn't terminal but sure puts a hitch in their lives, like Gabe Kincaid's.

It's not a brand new idea, but there's always room for one more kid on the block in this line of endeavor, and the hospital agreed that maybe Mike was just the guy to head this up.

Masterson called me about this thing himself. And he says he's calling all the other sports reporters as well. Most of them will probably hang up on him, thinking it's a prank call.

It's not a prank. If he has to talk to reporters and publicity people to get this done, then so be it. "You can't walk in there and talk to those kids and not do anything." He says it shaking his head, in disbelief that anyone could see what he's seen and not respond. So he's going to invite us all to respond with him.

Enter cosmic joke number three. I am making the first contribution to this grand enterprise. The hardened reporter who doesn't believe in anything is giving money to someone who's going to take little kids to Disney World. Ouch.

The punch line gets even better. Masterson has talked me into helping out with this thing. Like a fool, I said yes. I say like a fool because there's a little something old Bat doesn't know about me. I'd rather die than go into a hospital.

Still and all, I guess I'm going to have to get over that. Masterson's going to be hauling my tail into hospitals for months to come to promote his dream-come-true stuff.

There's plenty of room for the rest of you jokers to get in on this one on the ground floor. Masterson tells me this dream business is going to be expensive.

Promotions are already planned to get the ball rolling. One of the first will be a little pregame show a month from now pitting Masterson and his buddy Gabe Kincaid at catcher against a lineup of civic leaders. Having seen the mayor swing a bat, I'm betting on the kid with the unusual catching stance myself.

Masterson already has my check for $500. I gave it to him quickly before I chickened out. If I listened closely while I was writing it, there was laughter in the air. The whole thing has me looking over my shoulder, wondering if there's another punch line in store.

EIGHT

Meg came off the elevator quickly onto the third floor Wednesday morning. "How was your meeting with Harbison? What did he want?" Kim asked, looking up from her reports.

"My measurements," Meg said flatly, tossing a tape measure at her friend.

"Your measurements?" Kim's eyes widened and her head reared. "Something else you want to tell me? I mean, after all, he's married."

"No, not that way. For a uniform. A baseball uniform."

"For what?"

"For Masterson's benefit. I smell a rat."

"Oh?"

"Yeah." Meg paced around the nurses' station. "It seems the mayor has requested a player from the hospital for his team. Specifically, a female player. Naturally, I came to mind. Don't you hear Alex laughing about this someplace?"

195

Kim's brow wrinkled. "Could be. Is he on the team roster?"

Meg shook her head. "That's the aggravating part. The mayor's team is all city people and celebrities, no media, and Masterson's team is all ball players, and Gabe. I don't know where he's hiding, but Alex is out there someplace."

Kim patted her on the shoulder. "Maybe you're just paranoid. Maybe they just want you for your good looks and athletic ability. Can you hold a bat?"

"Oh, yeah, I can hold a bat. Use it, too. Alex engineered too many pickup games during college for me to not know how. We broke the manager's window in the radio station three different times."

Kim leaned back thoughtfully, threading the tape measure through her fingers. "So maybe he just did you a favor. I bet Harbison was pleased, anyway. Why don't we get these measurements?"

"Right," Meg said absently. Her brain was turning over everything rapidly, but nothing was making any sense. Alex had to have a hand in this.

That night over coffee, he looked shocked that she would mistrust him. "That's the full team roster?" she asked a third time.

"Honest, Maggie, the full roster. I will not be a player on that field."

"Okay, but I still think you had a hand in this, Alex. It would be just like you to get me roped into something with an audience of fifty thousand people."

"No, Maggie, not me. If I was going to put somebody in a tight uniform swinging a bat in front of fifty thousand people, I'd make sure it was someone who could hit.''

"Oh, that does it," she said, tossing her napkin down as Alex chortled. "I give up. But I just know you're involved in this somewhere."

"Hey, don't go away mad." He grabbed her arm as she slid out of the booth. The hamburger place halfway between the hospital and the station was getting to be their hangout. No one paid any attention to their boisterous conversations and squabbles anymore, especially not the staff. So when Alex slid over onto the seat, trapping Meg in, nobody batted an eye, even when he nuzzled her neck.

"Don't go away at all, at least not for a few minutes, okay?" His voice was soft and teasing. "I need to ask you a couple of questions. Gabe need help getting home tomorrow?"

"I don't think so. Spence is bringing the truck for all his stuff, and Martha said she'd drive the car over, too. That way he can ride in whatever he wants and be comfortable."

"He excited?"

Meg nodded. "And scared. I think he's the only one more hyper than me about this thing next week."

"Yeah, but he's got cause. If there are any scouts around, they won't be watching you, Maggie. They'll be watching our man Gabriel."

"And he knows it, Alex. I'll tell him you offered to help get him home. He'll get a kick out of that. For whatever perverse reasons, he enjoys your company."

"I kind of like his, too." Alex said, smiling. "He's the only other person in that hospital who appreciates a good joke."

"Well, if he appreciates any more with Kim Harris, your name is mud," Meg said, tracing a finger down his nose. He tossed his head back quickly and caught the tip of her finger between his teeth, flicking his tongue over it quickly before he released her.

"I could say I'd be good. Would she believe me?"

"Never in a million years. And if you don't hustle back to that station, you're going to be bad, and late."

"Yes, ma'am. Give me a good-bye kiss so I don't get any later than I already am."

"What a contradiction that is, Langdon. You know once I get started . . ." Still, she kissed him good-bye before he loped off into the dark and back to the television station to gather up the last of his material for the evening newscast.

The next morning Meg felt as if she was leading a parade. It seemed that half the junior class from Gabe's high school must have skipped school to help him load up the plants, the cards, the pictures, the paraphernalia of weeks in the hospital. A constant stream of giggling girls and boys with boxes went in and out of the room.

"I don't have the heart to invoke the regular visiting rules on them," Kim Harris admitted to Meg. They stood at the nurses' station watching the stream of kids. Liz Peters came out of Gabe's room and joined them, dodging two girls.

"You'll have to come downstairs when he goes

out," Meg told her friends, keeping her voice low. "One of the assistant principals called me about an hour ago. You won't believe what's going to go on down there."

"With Gabriel, anything is possible," Kim said, shaking her head. "He officially released yet?"

"They're in there now running over the instructions from the therapy department a final time," Liz said. "You're next."

"Good. I'll be glad to get in there, and out. This bevy of teenaged girls with different doses of perfume on is making me sneeze."

Meg grinned. "So that's what the tissues are for. Funny, I thought you might be getting sentimental in your old age."

"About as sentimental as your boyfriend's pets," Kim snapped, walking toward Gabe's room. "It will never happen."

Once Kim was gone, Meg turned to Liz. "Is this all going to work out all right?"

Liz nodded. "The graft took beautifully. Call it Masterson magic or whatever you like. I told him if he goes to PT over there like he's supposed to, there's no reason he shouldn't be playing in a month, even Legion ball if they'll let him. He's called the coach three times. The coach doesn't have a prayer."

Meg grinned. That was the Gabe she knew, the one that Mike and Alex had given back to her and Spence, and everyone. She watched as Gabe rolled out of the room, Spence pushing the wheelchair. "This is real dumb, Dad. They spend all this time getting me to walk straight, and I have to go out of here in this thing. Dumb.''

''For once, Gabriel, you will just have to do what they tell you,'' Spence said. ''I'm so glad to get you out of here, I'd put you on a skateboard if we needed to. Understood?''

Gabe rolled his eyes at Meg and sighed, asking silently for sympathy. ''Understood.''

Meg glanced over at Spence. If he had any idea of what was waiting outside, he didn't show it. They went down the elevator and the doors opened. Turning the corner into the main lobby, Meg could see them outside.

A few steps farther and Gabe could see them, too. ''What's going on out there?'' he asked, craning his neck. ''If that's what I think it is, we're slipping out the side door.''

''Oh, no, we're not, Gabe. Today we give them their way,'' Spence said. Meg could see the effort it was taking to keep his voice firm.

The big double doors whooshed open and Spence rolled the chair through, stopping about ten feet in front of them out in the spring sunshine. Meg could see the glints off Gabe's golden hair, and she put a hand on his arm, squeezing. She smiled when he looked up at her, and he smiled back.

The high school band was called the Lancers. They were dressed in Highland regalia that Meg supposed was hot in the sunshine.

The hospital's circular drive was filled with tall young men and women in kilts. With bagpipes. With trumpets and drums. A whistle was blown, and the drum major shouted. The ranks parted to make a wide path through the middle. The music started and Gabriel stood. Whenever she thought of him forever after, Meg saw him through a haze of tears she could not check, limping ever so slightly to a hero's march. It fit.

When it was all over and Gabe was next to the truck being pounded on the back and hooted and hollered over by his friends, Spence hugged her fiercely.

"Thanks for everything you've done for my boy."

"He deserved every bit of it," Meg said, walking over to ruffle Gabe's hair and say her farewells. When she saw him again, he wouldn't be a patient anymore but just another teenager like the dozen or so surrounding him, filling him in on the latest from sixth-period study hall. She fervently hoped it would always be that way.

Alex called in the afternoon, trying to weasel out of dinner for the first time in ten days. "Figured you might want to go home and chase dust bunnies," he said on the telephone.

"Figured wrong," Meg said. "I'll be working a little late at my desk, mostly stuff for Masterson's foundation. You can come by and we'll discuss it."

"Come by, as in stop by your desk?"

"That's the one."

He sounded tense. "Maggie, you're evil."

"No more evil than whoever put me up to playing ball with the mayor. See you at six."

At 6:05 the elevator opened and closed behind a pale Alex. Meg willed herself not to get up from her desk. She forced herself to sit behind it, watching him cross the hallway and come to where the partitions marked off her cubicle.

A sheen of sweat was on his forehead. "You made it. Good," she said, barely looking up. "This is the first time you've been up here alone, isn't it?"

"You know it is. I haven't been in any part of this hospital that didn't lead to Gabe's room for nearly two weeks."

"And look how far you've gotten," Meg said, really looking up for the first time. "You know, Alex, this foundation stuff means you're going to be in here. Not just with me, either. With Harbison, and some of the other folks. And you're going to make it."

His eyes had a gleam of bitterness. "Think I'll actually get to the point where I can regulate my breathing in the elevator?"

"I know you can. Just let go and try a little harder each time, okay?" She reached out and grasped one of his hands, squeezing it tightly.

He exhaled on a long, ragged note. "Okay, Maggie. For you."

"No, Alex. For you. For yourself. You have to take that kid that's inside of you and tell him it's okay to be afraid. But keep going anyway." She looked down, suddenly embarrassed. Using one finger, she pushed something over into his line of vision. "Here, read this."

He looked at the sheets of paper, flipping them as he read. "It's a proposal for a cable show about the hospital. So?"

"Keep reading."

He did, then looked up at her, eyes clear with surprise. "Who wrote this?"

"I did."

"While in your right mind? Maggie, this says you're going to host the thing."

Her chin jutted out. "You've been telling me I should kick this camera fright thing, and I decided you're right, Langdon. Let's chase the demons together, okay?"

His smile was slow in coming, but sweet when it came. "We'll give them hell together, Maggie. We really will."

It took Meg a moment to swallow the lump in her throat. When she did, she decided to ask plenty of questions. "Speaking of hell, Alex, what gives? I mean, I spend my days waiting for the other shoe to drop. Kim nearly lost it the other day when I had her open the box from the florist on a plastic sheet."

"And all you found were yellow roses." His smile was enchanting. It made Meg want to scream.

"This just isn't like you, Alex. Where's the catch?"

He leaned his forearms over the desk. "No catch. None whatsoever. Don't you really believe I can be this good, Maggie?"

"I believe you can be good," Meg countered, a slow smile spreading. "Just not this good, this way. I mean, you're even still fun." She grasped his hand, just inches from hers. It was warm and solid.

"I can be even more fun than this, Maggie. What kind of game do you want to play next?"

Meg tried not to sigh. It was all a game to Alex, in the end. "Let's just cut the games and eat dinner, all right?"

Alex seemed nonplussed. "Fine. Dinner. And I'll promise not to blow the paper off my straw."

"You're a prince among men, Alex," Meg murmured. It was just too bad he wasn't the kind of prince who was going to save the princess from her hospital tower.

The panic was rising so fast Meg was having trouble breathing. "Why am I doing this?" she muttered again, arranging her cap in the mirror. The face that looked back out at her looked about twelve. She was pale, freckles pushing out in dark relief all over. Her hair, caught back in a utilitarian ponytail, came out the back of the cap, holding it in place.

Now if her pulse would just stop racing and her hands shaking, maybe she'd be all right. For a moment she wished she hadn't ordered Alex to stay far, far away from her. "Don't you dare come down to those locker rooms or anywhere else near me," she'd warned.

"No locker rooms, I promise." Then why had there been that twinkle? Right now she could have used it, next to her, giving her some encouragement.

Instead, she pressed her lips together, trying to get them less dry, and headed for the door. The only other woman on the roster, an aide from the mayor's office, came out of a stall.

"These pants look right? They feel funny."

"They're fine," Meg said. On her they had some

shape. And the jersey seemed to be straining at the midpoint of the buttons. Funny, Meg hadn't noticed such problems. She shrugged it off and walked into the echoing concrete halls under the stadium.

She could hear the music playing and the crowd making noises outside. The Astroturf was so very green from down at this level, looking out. Someone in the home team uniform walked past her and did a double take.

"Meg? I mean Ms. Shepherd?" Gabe's arm went around her. It was a shock to realize just how tall he was, standing. "You look great."

She leaned into him, feeling some relief. "And you, Gabriel, look fantastic. How's the leg?"

"All right. I still have a funny stance, catching. Can't bend my leg all the way under me yet, so I cock it out to the side. Mike says some people actually catch that way on purpose." Gabe made a wry face that told her he wasn't going to be one of those people when he could do differently.

"Nervous?"

"A little. You?"

"Dying. I can't stand this kind of thing."

"You're kidding. I thought, with your job and all . . ."

Meg laughed, shakily. "You would think that, wouldn't you? But right now I'd give a month's salary not to have to go on the field."

"Oh, come on, Meg. It will be fun. And it will build character. Isn't that what you told me when you got me those video geometry lessons?"

"I guess so. How's that going, by the way?"

"Took their test. Didn't ace it but did well enough. I'm officially a senior in three weeks, just like everybody else."

She gave him a quick squeeze. "Good for you, Gabriel. Now wish me luck."

He pushed his cap back. "Are you kidding? I'm catching for the other guys, remember? How much luck you want me to give away?"

"Go. Catch good," she said, turning him toward the exit.

"Oh, I will. It's all I'll have to do when *some* people come up to bat," he said over his shoulder, laughing at her reaction.

In a moment they were all out on the field. Meg listened to the echo of the speeches on the loud-speaker, as the mayor gave the oversized check from the city to Masterson, as the crowd applauded, as Masterson made his speech about the foundation. It almost made her forget she was standing down in the lights.

Soon enough she remembered again. The mayor got up to bat. The mayor could not hit the broad side of a barn. The mayor didn't even get a walk, but he got some applause.

His aide, the one from the dressing room, got a single. The umpire, a large man, made a goofy show of waving her on to first base. The next person up, an alderman, popped up handily and Gabe caught the ball. Meg swelled with pride when the crowd roared for him. That was her boy.

"Next up, Meg Shepherd of Mercy Hospital."

Oh, nuts. Here it went. Meg's field of vision narrowed drastically. The bat boy handed her the lightest bat he had in his arsenal and she walked toward home plate. It looked a thousand miles away.

"Yes, sir, we've got a live one now, Michael," the umpire boomed. "See what you can do to strike out this one."

Oh, no. Oh, yes. Meg turned and looked at the official. He was extremely tall and broad shouldered in his dark gear. Where his handsome face was visible through the mask, his generous mouth was smiling, azure eyes twinkling.

"Alex, you promised!" Meg's heart was pounding so hard it felt as though it was taking a trip up into her throat. "You said you wouldn't be on this field."

He raised a finger and waggled it at her. "As a player. I am not a player, Maggie. I am an official. And if you stand here any longer talking, I'll get you for delaying the game."

"How do you expect me to turn my back on you?"

"I don't," he said calmly. "I expect you to turn sideways. You'll bat much better."

He stepped back, and Meg gave him a strangled growl. Of all the uncomfortable feelings she could imagine, batting with Alex Langdon behind her was the worst. At least Gabe was between them. Judging from his grin, he wasn't going to be much help if Alex got wild, though.

"Ball one," Alex roared and gestured. "Boy, Maggie, the view from back here is great. Turned profile like that, I can verify what I already know. Maggie, you have a teeny, tiny, little . . ."

"Alex . . ." she warned.

"Strike zone. Masterson has his work cut out for him. Turn around nice now, so he can throw again, Mutt."

Gabe whooped, and Meg felt herself getting a little dizzy. She focused on Masterson on the mound, who looked far away. Another pitch, and this time she swung.

"Strike one. Maggie, that was another ball. Just don't wave at them, okay?"

"Fine," she said through clenched teeth.

Ball two, and then ball three whirred past. "You've got him now, Maggie," Alex said with a chortle. "The mayor should have put more midgets on his team."

"Midgets!" Meg exploded. "Alex, I am not a midget. Five foot one may not be very tall, but I'm not a midget."

"Meg, he's getting to you," Gabe said, pushing up his mask.

"You're right, Gabriel." She jammed her cap on her head firmly and turned around, resolving not to look at Alex again.

Masterson got ready, fired, and another pitch went past. To Meg it looked like a strike, but she wasn't sure. She also wasn't going to turn around to give Alex the pleasure of giving her another hard time.

There was some laughter in the stands, and Meg wasn't sure why. Not until she dropped her bat as she was scooped up and tossed over Alex's shoulder. "I said ball, twice, Maggie. You're supposed to take your own base. But if you need help . . ."

She pounded on his back. "Put me down, now, Alex."

He was halfway down the baseline now, the crowd cheering him on. "Put you down? But we're a hit, here, Maggie."

"I'm going to hit you all right, Langdon. Put me down before I have a full-fledged panic attack before fifty thousand people."

"Now why should I put you down just because you're a little panicky?" He patted her posterior.

"Because when I have a panic attack, Langdon, first I hyperventilate, then I throw up."

He put her down, quickly. They were nearly at the base anyway. Alex got a whisk broom out of one of the many large pockets of his jacket and ceremoniously dusted off first base. The baseman was nearly on the ground, doubled over with laughter. With a burning sensation rising in her face, Meg realized it was the same guy who'd been in the whirlpool with Masterson. The one without the tan briefs.

Alex made a courtly wave onto the base. "I'm sorry if I embarrassed you. But admit it, it was fun."

"It was not," she called to his retreating back. She balled her fists, willing herself not to cry or scream or anything. The trembling in her legs calmed enough that she wasn't afraid they were going to give way.

And when she looked over at the first baseman, he had the good grace not to laugh. His lips twitched, but he didn't laugh. "You going to steal on me? Should I be on my toes here?"

"I ought to try to steal just to get away from

you," Meg muttered. At that moment there was a crack and the ball went sailing for the outfield. A player was under it before Meg got halfway to second, and her half of the inning was mercifully over. "Even Langdon can't get to me in right field," she said to no one in particular.

Right field was very peaceful. Meg even found herself cheering for Gabe when he hit one of the mayor's few on-target pitches and got a single. The way the benefit was rigged, it was to their advantage for Masterson's team to get a run or two anyway. The mayor had rashly wagered that he'd keep them scoreless for the whole inning of play. Meg hoped he did better at legislating than at ball playing.

The first baseman with the wicked grin brought Gabe home with a powerful triple. The mayor let his aide pitch for a couple batters, and she actually struck one out. The alderman in left field caught a pop fly, and things were down to Bat Masterson.

Meg breathed a sigh of relief. Alex had behaved, staying behind the plate, even shaking Gabe's hand after he crossed the bag. Then her mouth went very dry. She watched Masterson at the plate. He batted left-handed.

Now why, in all the time she'd been listening to Gabe, hadn't that registered? So much for her peaceful position in right field. It took only two pitches, and there she was, planning to be the goat. The ball seemed to stay in the air forever while she danced around under it, trying to get into position.

It plummeted down and landed, unbelievably, in her glove. Masterson stopped rounding the bases and headed for the dugout. Meg was so dumbfounded, looking at the glove that she didn't see the large, dark shape bearing down on her until it got there. Alex picked her up and whirled her around once and put her down, kissing her firmly.

All of Meg's panic balled itself into one action. Alex never saw it coming until it connected. She drew back and slapped him, enjoying the sting in her palm as she hit his cheek. Meg didn't look back as she strode from the field. She wouldn't have been able to see for the tears if she'd turned back anyway.

Meg sat at a picnic table listening to the game drone on the loudspeakers carrying the radio play-by-play for fans buying hot dogs and peanuts. She gave a sigh and a shudder, finished with the crying jag. In place of the tears a monumental dose of anger was percolating up through her spine, straightening her posture on the hard bench.

"He's looking all over for you," Spence said calmly, handing her his handkerchief again. Meg took it, wondering how many of these Martha had laundered her mascara off by now.

"Let him look, self-satisfied bastard. I'm never speaking to him again." She took off the cap and smoothed it in her hands.

"Really? After all of this, you're done with him."

"Done," she said firmly, looking up at Spence. "He's humiliated me for the last time."

"Was it that much of a humiliation, then? Having a man you love so proud of you he kissed you in front of fifty thousand people? And he's supposed to

be a neutral observer, too." Spence said, a grin playing with one corner of his mouth.

"Love?" Meg tried to sound brittle. "Now why
would you use that word?"

"I'm a twenty-year veteran of marriage, Meg. It
shows."

"Come on, Spence. I was dying out there. All I
wanted to do was crawl in some hole. Some nice,
quiet, comfortable hole."

"Did you? Did you even remember you were nervous while Alex was around?"

She looked at the floor beneath her. The pitted
concrete under the picnic table at the family snack
area wasn't very interesting. But it beat her painful
recollections. "Not really. I guess while he was
around I forgot for a few minutes."

"You usually do, don't you? Forget everything
else. Tell me, Margaret, that it isn't that way."
Spence took her hands and made her look into his
sunburned face, the wrinkles around his eyes gathering into tight lines. "Tell me that everything else
doesn't melt away when he walks up to you."

She looked away, to the families with shrieking
children getting a last snack before the game got
serious.

"You can't, can you? I've seen you two. It's the
same as I remember, some twenty-odd years ago. I
went through an entire dance once with mismatched
socks. Had no idea one was black and one was
brown because I was with the most beautiful girl in
four counties."

Meg wiped her cheek one more time with his

handkerchief and watched Spence. He was looking at a father picking up a little redheaded girl, but she knew he saw neither of them. He saw a young woman, with blond hair and a compact figure who was still there underneath the Martha Kincaid Meg knew. He went on. "She still is, you know. The prettiest girl in four counties. I tell her so, and she whomps me with a dish towel. But she knows. And you know too, don't you, Meg? Is it worth it, this pride?"

"I've got to keep my pride, Spence. He can't just go on making a fool of me."

"Funny, I would have said he was making a fool of himself over you this time," Spence said. "He was being pretty goofy out there to entertain you. And it did take your mind off things. And he's not going to change."

No, he wasn't. He was going to remain Alex, brash and brave and wicked. And suddenly Meg wanted to find him more than anything in the world. She looked up, and Spence smiled. "He's in the company box. Said to give you this if you wanted it," he said, pulling a ticket out the pocket of his plaid shirt. "Now go."

She went. When the usher let her into the box, Alex looked up, blue eyes startled. "Never mind, okay?" he said into the telephone he was holding and put it down. "You're here."

"I'm here," Meg said, smoothing her cap between her fingers. Now she wished she'd changed into something more presentable. Alex didn't seem to notice. He took her by the arm and ushered her to the outdoor portion of the box.

"Alex, what's he doing here?"

"That's Stu. He's my cameraman," Alex said, as if having a man with a video camera on a tripod was something everyone did at the ball game.

"I know that. Hello, Stu." Stu gave her a wave and went back to watching the game as he leaned over the railing at the corner of the box. "But why is he here?"

"I'm working. We're doing the news breaks at eight and at nine unless the city blows up."

"Great. You can talk and I'll stand out in the hall," Meg said with a shiver.

Alex put an arm around her. "You don't have to do that. I'd really like you here, especially for the nine o'clock one. I won't make you say a thing."

"And you won't embarrass me or anything?" Meg asked, looking up into his shining eyes.

"I'll certainly try not to." He nuzzled into her neck gently for a moment. "I wouldn't ever do anything intentionally just to embarrass you."

His eyes were clear and innocent as a babe's. "You wouldn't, would you?" Meg said, stroking his cheek. The skin was smooth and taut over his cheekbone and nubby lower down where his beard started. Both textures made her fingers tingle. "I'm sorry about slapping you on the field, then."

"I had it coming. I should be more gentle with you, Maggie. You're not meant for all the hooliganism I've put you through. Still love me?"

"Still love you," she said, letting her hand rest

on the nape of his neck. She waited for an admission from Alex, but it didn't come. Instead, he leaned down and took a long, slow kiss. Meg could hear Stu whistling at the rail.

"Do me a favor?"

Meg looked at him. Alex looked tense, and she wanted to ease that tension. "Sure. What?"

"Take down your hair."

Wordlessly she took the band out of her ponytail and shook it free in a wavy cascade. Alex sighed. "Better. Want to help me fill out the scorecard?" Alex asked when he'd settled back into his chair.

"Have you forgotten who you're talking to?"

"Not at all. I just thought you might want to learn."

Meg thought about all the baseball games she would probably see in her lifetime. There would be the ones that Alex reported on, the ones he wrote about, the ones he saw on his day off. There would even be some, further down the line, where they could both sit on hard wooden bleachers and watch someone in size six baseball pants round the bases. Perhaps it was time to learn to fill out a scorecard.

By the fifth inning she had most of it down pat. Then Masterson stole a base and she realized she had no idea what kind of a sign to use. "Alex?" she asked, looking over to where he was standing near the corner of the box, stretching his legs.

He raised a hand. "Not now." Then Stu was in front of him and quickly, flawlessly, he recapped the game so far in thirty seconds. A light flashed on the camera, Stu relaxed, and they chatted during a commercial at the station. Alex came back on for a few moments, smiled brilliantly at the end, and stepped aside. Stu went to refill his drink.

Alex got a bag of peanuts and they shared them. Meg shivered at the sensuality of his salty fingers as he fed her the peanuts, one by one.

They watched the game, and she wondered where Alex's usual intensity for the sport was. He seemed to be keyed up, but not about the game. Even when she showed him her scorecard, he was congratulatory but vague.

"Part of it is missing, here in the fifth," he pointed out.

"I had a little trouble during your report. About your report, Alex. It was . . . elegant, I'd say." Meg curled an arm around him.

"Thank you. Coming from you, I'd consider it the highest of compliments," Alex said. He tilted his head back, looking up into the dark sky above them. "No, I'd say that was almost the highest compliment."

"There's higher? Knowing you, I'd say thinking you did your job well would be as high as you could get."

"Not quite. I'd like to think I was an elegant friend and lover and the like. If you can tell me I do that job well, that would be the highest compliment, Maggie." He took her hand and kissed it un-self-consciously. "So how come you don't have Masterson's stolen base on this scorecard?"

"Didn't know the sign. But I'm sure you'll be more than happy to enlighten me."

"SB."

Meg laughed. "It's that simple? I figured the same guy who decided that strikeouts ought to be a K figured it out and it would be something esoteric."

Alex shook his head. "It's that simple. Kind of like loving you, Maggie. Simple and natural, and totally terrifying."

Her head was whirling. "Loving me, Alex?"

He nodded solemnly. "Loving you. I don't know how long I've known, but it's been a while. And it's more terrifying than walking in a hospital."

Meg found her throat constricting. "Truly?"

He nodded. "Truly. How am I ever going to do it all right?"

"You don't have to do it all right, Alex. Just give it your best shot, okay?" He drew her to him. Alex honestly looked nervous. "This your way of proposing or something?"

"No, not yet. Let me straighten my tie for that."

Meg got a frisson of excitement. "Fine." He straightened his tie and put an arm around her shoulders. Looking at her, Alex rearranged a strand of hair.

"I'm glad you slipped off the uniform shirt. The T-shirt looks better. Okay, here goes."

Meg was looking just at Alex, only at Alex. He was so keyed up that she was willing him to calm down, wanted to reach out and smooth the tenseness out of his forehead, still the uneasiness she saw in his tight shoulders. It was only when what he was saying with that adorable mouth really registered that she realized this was not just a private event.

"This is Alex Langdon, and we're here during the seventh-inning stretch for an important announcement. With me is Ms. Mary Margaret Shepherd, and we're about to find out if she's crazy enough to marry me. Well, Maggie, what do you think? You game?"

Meg should have seen it coming. Only Alex could have engineered this. Before she could answer, she heard a roar from the crowd and realized that this little transmission was also on the computerized scoreboard. Before she could react to a four-foot-high version of her own face, a little cartoon graphic flashed on the screen. The little guy on his knees had a balloon above his head saying "Marry me, Maggie."

Alex was back for a moment. "We'll be back with an answer after this brief message."

The light on the camera flicked off. "How brief, Langdon? Long enough for me to kill you?"

Alex shook his head as he reached under the seat. "Not even long enough to find the chocolate-covered solitaire in this container of chocolate-covered raisins. Just quick enough for an answer, Maggie. Forty-five seconds, and sixteen of them are gone already."

Forty-five seconds to decide whether or not to marry Alex. Below in the stands Maggie could hear distinct voices. "Some of those people say I'd be crazy to marry you, Alex."

"What do you say, Maggie?" His face was so intense, almost pleading. It amazed her that Alex truly didn't know the answer already.

"I'd be crazy. But I'm going to do it anyway. I love you, Alex Langdon, even with this kind of craziness. My acceptance does not preclude my killing you once we get off the air."

"I figured that. I love you so much, Maggie, I wanted everybody to know."

The phone rang inside and he bolted, lunging for it. "Yes," he said into it and hung up.

The light flickered on the camera. "She said yes. I'm doomed but very happy. Alex Langdon, KTIX Sports."

Stu focused down on the scoreboard again where little fireworks in different colors were going off around a big "SHE SAID YES."

"I'm not going to kill you, Alex," Meg said, nuzzling into the side of his neck. "I'm going to let you live until I can find a suitable way to pay you back for this delightful event, which I will remember for the rest of our lives."

He turned his head to her, oblivious of Stu, who was packing up his equipment and pretending to be invisible. "You'll never top this one."

"Oh, no?" It was hard to keep the giggles out of her voice.

Alex drew his head back. "You witch. You've already got something in mind."

Meg's giggles escaped like little spurts of pressure on a steam valve. "Let's just say Masterson has some real creative stuff planned for promotions. He's discovered your florist."

Alex leaned his head back, looking up at the

lights. "Oh, no. Let me guess. He's going to do something with those cow pies."

"Attractively boxed, with a message of your choice," Meg said. "He's just looking for a suitable victim so that he can sell shares to fill their office to the ceiling."

Alex groaned. "If everybody who has ever been the brunt of one of my jokes bought just one. . . . That does it. I'm encasing both of my offices in plastic sheeting before we go away on our honeymoon." He turned to look at Meg, and she drank in the love she saw in his eyes. "Where are we going, anyway?"

"I don't know yet. But once we decide, it's a state secret. From now on, our personal affairs are just that. Personal, got it?" She tugged his thick dark blond hair for emphasis.

"Hey, Maggie, even I have my limits. I can be a very private person when I want to be. And right now, I want to be." The door clicked closed behind Stu. There was a crack of cowhide on wood down below and the crowd roared. Alex never stopped kissing her.

"I think someone just hit a home run," she said breathlessly as he meandered down to the hollow of her throat.

"Somebody else can keep track tonight. I've got a different game in mind."

"Do we have to call it on account of darkness?"

"We won't call in on account of anything, Maggie." he said tenderly, murmuring into her ear. "It will go on forever."

"I've already got my nominee for most valuable player," she said softly, letting the scorecard slide out of her lap and onto the floor of the box. "Star of the game."

"Do I get a wristwatch and a convertible?"

"Even better. You get me, and I get you. But Alex, there's still a lot I don't know, besides filling out scorecards."

"I've never seen a more promising rookie," he said, with a heavy, hazy smile. "I'll never need anyone else on my team. Forever, Maggie?"

"Forever, Alex." The kiss that sealed her vow lifted Meg's heart over the fence in the outfield, right at the four-hundred-foot mark. It sailed out into the starlit darkness, going, going, gone.

SHARE THE FUN . . .
SHARE YOUR NEW-FOUND TREASURE!!

You don't want to let your new books out of your sight?
That's okay. Your friends can get their own. Order below.

No. 108 IN YOUR DREAMS by Lynn Bulock
Meg's dreams become reality when Alex reappears in her peaceful life.

No. 45 PERSONAL BEST by Margaret Watson
Nick is a cynic; Tess, an optimist. Where does love fit in?

No. 46 ONE ON ONE by JoAnn Barbour
Vincent's no saint but Loie's attracted to the devil in him anyway.

No. 47 STERLING'S REASONS by Joey Light
Joe is running from his conscience; Sterling helps him find peace.

No. 48 SNOW SOUNDS by Heather Williams
In the quiet of the mountain, Tanner and Melaine find each other again.

No. 49 SUNLIGHT ON SHADOWS by Lacey Dancer
Matt and Miranda bring out the sunlight in each other's lives.

No. 50 RENEGADE TEXAN by Becky Barker
Rane lives only for himself—that is, until he meets Tamara.

No. 51 RISKY BUSINESS by Jane Kidwell
Blair goes undercover but finds more than she bargained for with Logan.

No. 52 CAROLINA COMPROMISE by Nancy Knight
Richard falls for Dee and the glorious Old South. Can he have both?

No. 53 GOLDEN GAMBLE by Patrice Lindsey
The stakes are high! Who has the winning hand—Jessie or Bart?

No. 54 DAYDREAMS by Marina Palmieri
Kathy's life is far from a fairy tale. Is Jake her Prince Charming?

No. 55 A FOREVER MAN by Sally Falcon
Max is trouble and Sandi wants no part of him. She *must* resist!

No. 56 A QUESTION OF VIRTUE by Carolyn Davidson
Neither Sara nor Cal can ignore their almost magical attraction.

No. 57 BACK IN HIS ARMS by Becky Barker
Fate takes over when Tara shows up on Rand's doorstep again.

No. 58 SWEET SEDUCTION by Allie Jordan
Libby wages war on Will—she'll win his love yet!

No. 59 13 DAYS OF LUCK by Lacey Dancer
Author Pippa Weldon finds her real-life hero in Joshua Luck.

No. 60 SARA'S ANGEL by Sharon Sala
Sara must get to Hawk. He's the only one who can help.

No. 61 HOME FIELD ADVANTAGE by Janice Bartlett
Marian shows John there is more to life than just professional sports.

No. 62 FOR SERVICES RENDERED by Ann Patrick
Nick's life is in perfect order until he meets Claire!

No. 63 WHERE THERE'S A WILL by Leanne Banks
Chelsea goes toe-to-toe with her new, unhappy business partner.

No. 64 YESTERDAY'S FANTASY by Pamela Macaluso
Melissa always had a crush on Morgan. Maybe dreams do come true!

No. 65 TO CATCH A LORELEI by Phyllis Houseman
Lorelei sets a trap for Daniel but gets caught in it herself.

No. 66 BACK OF BEYOND by Shirley Faye
Dani and Jesse are forced to face their true feelings for each other.

No. 67 CRYSTAL CLEAR by Cay David
Max could be the end of all Chrystal's dreams . . . or just the beginning!
